MISTLETOE BABY MIX-UP

JC HARROWAY

Harlequin

MEDICAL ROMANCE

H Harlequin®
MEDICAL ROMANCE

ISBN-13: 978-1-335-99337-3

Mistletoe Baby Mix-Up

Copyright © 2025 by JC Harroway

H Harlequin Enterprises ULC
22 Adelaide St. West, 41st Floor
Toronto, Ontario M5H 4E3, Canada
www.Harlequin.com

HarperCollins Publishers
Macken House, 39/40 Mayor Street Upper,
Dublin 1, D01 C9W8, Ireland
www.HarperCollins.com

Printed in U.S.A.

She was having a baby. Another man's baby.

This...*thing* with Théo, whatever it was, should be the last thing on her mind.

Théo smiled but there was no warmth in the expression. Only malice and fury and that heated kind of hunger she wasn't sure was real or a figment of her hormonal imagination.

"Because I too spoke to Mr. Roulet this morning," he said, glancing down at her stomach.

Connie placed her hand there to shield the baby from his anger.

"And from what he said," Théo went on, his icy tone in stark contrast to the flames in his eyes, "I'm almost one hundred percent certain that your baby is also mine."

Dear Reader,

If you are anything like me, you still believe in the magic of Christmas.

Helping Connie and Théo to find each other and fall in love against the backdrop of the festive season was an absolute joy!

I hope you enjoy reading their journey from two people burned by love and scared to risk their hearts to a happy-ever-after family.

Love,

JC x

Lifelong romance addict **JC Harroway** took a break from her career as a junior doctor to raise a family and found her calling as a Harlequin author instead. She now lives in New Zealand and finds that writing feeds her very real obsession with happy endings and the endorphin rush they create. You can follow her at jcharroway.com and on Facebook, X and Instagram.

Books by JC Harroway

Harlequin Medical Romance

A Sydney Central Reunion

Phoebe's Baby Bombshell

Buenos Aires Docs

Secretly Dating the Baby Doc

Jet Set Docs

One Night to Sydney Wedding

Royally Tempted

One Night to Royal Baby

Sexy Surgeons in the City

Manhattan Marriage Reunion

Nurse's Secret Royal Fling
Forbidden Fiji Nights with Her Rival
The Midwife's Secret Fling

Visit the Author Profile page
at Harlequin.com for more titles.

To Mum, thanks for all the Christmas magic.

CHAPTER ONE

Four weeks to Christmas

SPINAL SURGEON CONNIE DUBOIS tucked a stray lock of hair under her surgical hat as she left the theatre changing rooms, energised to be back at work after two days of absence. As she sailed along the corridor, smiling at passing colleagues, she hugged her precious secret to her like a warm, cosy blanket. She'd finally taken control of her personal life and all that was left to do was simply wait and wonder if the intrauterine insemination procedure she'd undergone two days ago might have worked. She could be pregnant right now, not that a pregnancy test would turn positive for a week or more.

Connie headed for her designated operating room for her full day of surgeries ahead. When her phone rang with a call from her best friend, Tristan, she picked up.

'How did it go?' he asked, his voice full of cautious optimism. Wonderful Tris had offered to be her sperm donor so she could have a child all by herself.

'Good. But I'm glad to be back at work.' She rested a hand on her flat stomach and inhaled through the flutter of premature excitement and anticipation.

She'd always wanted a child. Of course, she'd assumed that by the age of thirty-five she might have found the love of her life with whom to have a baby, but that hadn't panned out. Her former fiancé had proved himself a liar and a cheat. The only other man with potential, Tristan's brother Théo... Well, he'd been another massive mistake she regretted.

'Any second thoughts?' Tris asked hesitantly.

'No regrets,' she said, decisively. She didn't need a man in her life. Or love, or even sex. She was a determined and capable professional woman who could and would do this alone.

'How about you and Victor?' she asked about Tristan's soon-to-be husband. Neither he nor Victor wanted children of their own. But all three of them had done their homework and brainstormed the pros and cons of their unconventional decision before proceeding.

'No regrets here either,' Tris said. 'I'm just glad the procedure wasn't too awful for you. Listen, Con... I, um, have something to tell you...'

In that moment, Connie arrived at the theatre

reception desk and handed over her pager so it could be answered while she was operating.

'Okay.' Connie glanced at the clock on the wall and winced. 'I'll call you later though, after my surgery. I'm about to scrub in and I'm running late.' Knowing Tristan, who was also a doctor at the same hospital, would understand that patients always came first, she disconnected the call and gave the receptionist instructions to field any urgent enquiries to Connie's registrar, Jules.

In theatre ten's scrub room, she reached for a mask from a box on the wall, her mind turning to the busy day of spinal surgeries ahead. Fortunately she loved her job, so wasn't daunted by the prospect of the long and complex surgery she was about to perform with a colleague. And her patient, sixteen-year-old Elodie, had been preying on Connie's mind. The young woman's severe scoliosis had begun to impinge on her breathing. She deserved a life free of pain and physical limitation.

Connie had just raised the mask to her face when the door squeaked open at her back. Expecting it to be Dr Bedeau, the surgical colleague assisting her with this morning's surgery, she turned to greet the man with a warm smile.

Shock snatched at her breath. Her arms fell limply to her sides as she took in the surgeon who'd arrived instead: Théo Augustin, Tristan's older brother.

'What on earth are you doing here?' she asked, stunned and more than a little embarrassed to see the man she disliked almost as much as her ex-fiancé at *her* hospital. And how dared he be just as sexy as when she'd last seen him three years ago?

Tall, broad-shouldered, with untamed dark brown hair and coffee-coloured eyes, he oozed sex appeal and confidence, flooding Connie's body with heat and hormones and inconvenient memories of the night she'd stupidly let down her guard and slept with him after too much champagne. It had been lust at first sight when they'd met at *le réveillon de Noël*, the Christmas Eve party at his Paris apartment. Every time she'd sought him out with her eyes that evening, he'd been looking at her, the sexual tension building to frantic levels. When Tristan had headed to bed after the guests had left, she'd offered to load the glasses into the dishwasher and she and Théo had kissed before tearing into each other's clothes, right there in the kitchen.

But they'd both instantly regretted that one night of rebound sex—well, in Connie's case, *almost* instantly. It had taken the humiliation of overhearing Théo express his regrets the next morning to shunt Connie from post-best-sex-of-her-life dream state to one-night-stand remorse.

'Dr Dubois,' he said, his bold stare sweeping over her and his sexy deep voice buzzing at her eardrums like the irritating drone of a chainsaw. 'Good to see you again.'

With her body on fire from humiliation and rejecting his easy-going smile that stretched his sexy mouth and flashed his straight white teeth, Connie watched in horror as he joined her at the sinks without further explanation. He reached for his own mask, confidently tying it on as if he were about to scrub in. On *her* surgery.

'This is *my* OR,' Connie pointed out, still gaping at him in disbelief. 'You must be in the wrong place, the wrong hospital even.'

Had he hit his head and suffered memory loss? He worked at Paris University Hospital, not here at St Raphaël. And despite that one foolish mistake they'd made three years ago, despite Connie's close relationship with Tris, she'd deliberately gone out of her way to avoid this man. But now he was in her face, too close, too hot, too... utterly infuriating even though he'd only spoken a handful of words.

'Haven't you heard?' he asked, shooting her a quizzical look before starting the flow of water to commence his hand-washing routine. As if he were the surgeon in charge. 'I'm assisting you today. The Elodie Verdier case.' Théo shrugged and Connie caught a whiff of his delicious cologne.

'Elodie Verdier is *my* patient,' she snapped, quickly tying on her mask to block out the sexy scent of him, which only flooded her brain with more erotic memories.

'Right,' he said, unfazed, opening a fresh scrubber and lathering up his strong muscular forearms with iodine suds, his movements automatic. 'Sixteen-year-old with a fifty-three-degree thoracic scoliosis, shortness of breath and impaired lung functions tests. I'm up to speed on the case. I met the patient yesterday and reviewed the scans while you were absent.'

Despite the mask covering most of his face, she could tell he was smiling that sexy and charming smile of his. She might still find him attractive, but she'd changed in the past three years. When they'd met her confidence had been at an all-time low after she'd dumped her cheating ex, Guy, six months before.

'But you don't work here,' she pointed out, icy panic sliding through her veins.

'I do as of today,' he said, calmly. 'I've been headhunted to lead spinal surgery at St Raphaël. We'll be working together from now on. Didn't Chief of Surgery let you know?'

'No…' she muttered, in shock. She couldn't deny that he was a good surgeon, or so she'd heard. But working together?

Théo frowned as if frustrated. 'I was aware my acceptance of the role might cause some… awkwardness, given we slept together,' he said, his stare lingering for a fraction too long, as if he too was remembering that passionate night. 'But the promotion was too good an opportunity to pass up, I'm afraid. Besides, we're both professional adults. I assumed we could leave the past behind.' He worked the scrubber over his hands and under his nails as he spoke. 'If the positions were reversed, I'd hope you wouldn't overlook a promotion simply to avoid me.'

'I can't believe this…' Connie muttered, her doubts building as she processed his words. 'Why didn't Tris warn me about you?'

Unless this had been what her friend had wanted to tell her earlier when she'd been in a hurry and preoccupied with the possible pregnancy.

'That's my fault,' he said with regret. 'I asked Tris to hold off telling you until I knew for sure I wanted to accept the position, which was yesterday. Then it all happened so quickly. They asked me to start right away and I had some annual leave accrued at my former position so I could.'

'But…where's Dr Bedeau?' Connie asked in desperation, determined to be immune to Théo's charms as she fumbled over opening her own scrub brush and tossed the packaging in the bin. This was why she struggled to take time off work. It was easy to lose touch with the goings-on at the hospital and clearly something monumental had occurred while she'd been absent. Théo Augustin had happened!

But she didn't want to operate with Théo Augustin. She didn't want to look at him, talk to him or even think about him. She certainly didn't want to recall that amazing night and the resulting humiliation of the morning after when she'd overheard him voice his regrets they'd slept together to Tristan. Him casting her aside after rebound sex had brought up all the freshly scabbed-over pain of Guy's betrayal and rejection.

Of course, smarting from what her ex had done—lied, cheated and impregnated the other woman—Connie should have known better than to expect anything else from a man...

'Dr Bedeau had some scheduling conflicts today,' Théo said reasonably. 'When he found out I would be leading the team, he asked me to step in for him. I am quite good at this surgery stuff, you know. No need to look so horrified.'

Connie looked away from his smiling eyes and waved her hand at the sensor to activate the flow of water from her tap, unready to accept his attempts to lighten the mood. 'Don't you think, as a courtesy, consultant to consultant, you should have let me know you'd be assisting with my patient?'

She scrubbed at her nails, desperate now to claw back control of her surgery. 'When it comes to my professional life,' she added, 'I'm afraid I demand honesty and full transparency. So if you plan on working with me, that's something to bear in mind.'

'I did try,' he said, glancing her way with a frown. 'I didn't know you'd be absent. I spoke with Jules, your junior, yesterday on the ward. Didn't he tell you?'

'No.' Connie lathered up her arms and hands, scrubbing so vigorously her skin tingled.

She hadn't had chance to catch up with her registrar yet this morning. And the date for the insemination procedure had been last minute and unplanned to coincide with ovulation.

But why was this happening to her? She'd arrived at work earlier, cradling the possibility of a pregnancy, glad to be back and eager to perform Elodie's surgery. But now she needed to contend with the resurfaced humiliation of that night, her stubborn sexual attraction to the man and awkwardness of having him as a colleague.

'By the way,' he said. 'I'm always honest and transparent.'

Connie gaped under her mask. Him, always honest? Not in her experience, but then now wasn't the time for personal conversations.

'Is there some unfinished business between us that I'm unaware of?' he continued in that reasonable tone that only wound her tighter. 'I assumed not, given the way things ended.'

'None whatsoever,' she lied, because he was the last person to whom she wanted to show any hint of vulnerability, especially at work. 'As far as I'm concerned, you and I never happened. It was so forgettable.'

He nodded, his stare disbelieving and his eyes crinkling in the corners as he smiled under the mask. 'Yes, you made your regret pretty clear the next morning. Fleeing without so much as a goodbye and ignoring me ever since.'

Connie scrubbed her hands harder. 'The past is the past.' She was focussed on the future. *Her* future, motherhood, a baby.

'All I care about,' she continued, aware of his eyes on her, 'is that you're muscling in on my surgery. This is my patient and I never asked for your help.'

'Some would consider my help and experience invaluable, Connie,' he scoffed, then stepped back from the sink and held his dripping-wet arms before him, his hand-washing complete. 'Why don't we, as you suggest, put the past behind us and find some way of working together?'

Connie bit her tongue. He was the more experienced surgeon. His expertise was a good thing for Elodie. She could swallow down her pride and dislike and behave professionally at work for the sake of her patients. And if he'd been invited to take the surgical lead in her department, she'd have no choice but to interact with him. That didn't mean she and Théo Augustin would be having any sort of personal relationship. Not even friends.

'Fine,' she said finally, caught between a rock and a hard place. 'I'll tolerate your assistance on this one occasion.' With Dr Bedeau absent, she unfortunately needed Théo's help. She could definitely use her distrust to counter the fact that she still fancied him. 'But don't make a habit of sneaking into my surgeries without first speaking to me,' she warned.

'Noted,' he said with a nod. After a moment's rapt fascination, where he stared as if he had more to say, he pushed at the door with his back and entered the operating room to gown up.

Connie slowly exhaled, her adrenaline fading. Trying to shove Théo and the memories he ignited from her mind, she focussed on cleaning her hands, her joyously optimistic and potentially life-changing morning washed away like suds down the drain.

CHAPTER TWO

GOWNED UP AND revved up, Théo held his sterile gloved hands in front of him, waiting for Connie to appear in the operating room. These past three years since they slept together, he'd only seen her in photographs with Tristan. But in person, she looked good. *Really* good. Of course, she was also still eager to avoid him. Still cryptic and unfriendly. Still way too sexy…

But trying to pretend as if that night hadn't happened? Was she kidding? Théo had done his best over the years to forget, but no matter how deep his own regrets over the poor timing—he'd slept with Connie Dubois when he was still grieving the death of his brief and tumultuous marriage— forgetting about that night and sex that hot would be a struggle.

Théo sighed. Clearly whatever regrets she'd had after sleeping with him were still very much alive. He'd feared as much, the reason he'd hesitated over taking the job at St Raphaël. But his career had become the second most important thing in his life after Tris. And he truly hoped he and Connie could lay the past to rest.

She appeared from the scrub room, slipping into sterile gown and gloves with the assistance of a scrub nurse. Before he could speak to her again, to try and smooth things over because he could appreciate her dislike of being caught off guard by his sudden appearance, the anaesthetised patient was wheeled in.

While the patient was draped in sterile sheets and attached to the various machines the anaesthetist would use to monitor her, Théo once more tried to make peace.

'Look, I'm sorry that you weren't expecting me,' he said, frustrated that his attraction to her hadn't diminished in the slightest, despite her reception being as frosty as the cold and empty bed he'd returned to that morning three years ago. 'Maybe I should have warned you sooner. But we're about to spend the next few hours operating together.'

Other apologies formed on his tongue as he observed her rigid posture and haughty silence. He should never have slept with her so soon after his divorce. Should never have slept with anyone, least of all a good friend of his brother's. He'd still been emotionally reeling from the failure of his marriage and the dashed hopes of having a family of his own. Of course, the moment he'd met Connie, he'd reeled for a whole other reason—

instant, intense and unexpected attraction. The next morning, despite a great night, he'd realised he still wasn't ready for any sort of relationship, which was exactly what he'd planned to tell Connie. Only he'd never had the chance to explain himself or ask her what she expected or let her down gently. She'd left his place without saying goodbye to him or Tris, who'd brought her along to the party, and ignored Théo's texts. Théo had tried to summon up relief that she'd left before they'd had a chance to talk, but for some reason all he'd felt was hollow and guilty.

'Which is why I think it's best if we leave our personal stuff at the door, don't you?' Connie said, stiffly, as if it were anything but fine.

'I agree,' he said, wondering again what she'd meant by all that cloak and dagger stuff about honesty and transparency.

'Good. Let's start, shall we?' Connie said as the theatre technicians manipulated the unconscious patient into the correct position, lying on her side.

As they began the surgery, Théo was eager to discover what kind of surgeon Connie was. 'Are you tethering over spinal fusion?' he asked about the possible corrective procedure for scoliosis that involved a chain of screws placed into the individual vertebrae, which were then connected by a wire under tension that helped to realign the abnormal curvature.

'Yes,' she said, casting him another wary look. 'Why? What would you do?'

Théo stifled a sigh at her defensiveness. 'I'd do the same in this case. It wasn't a trick question, Connie. Have you seen the cutting-edge approaches to scoliosis surgery coming out of Denmark?'

'I've read a few papers on the Holm technique,' she said, casting him a dismissive look as she readied the surgical instruments she'd need.

Théo nodded, impressed that she was across the emerging surgical approaches. 'I've performed it a couple of times,' he said. 'I'd be happy to lead you through it some time.' But his offer was met only with a terse and dismissive nod.

For the next thirty minutes, they worked together in near silence. Considering Connie hadn't been expecting him, nor was he her favourite person, Théo was impressed by how readily they set aside their personal issues and collaborated. With the patient on single lung ventilation—a technique that intentionally collapsed one lung to facilitate visibility of the thoracic spine—they readied the thoracoscope, a camera they could pass into the chest through a small incision between the ribs to visualise the misaligned thoracic vertebrae. The minimally invasive technique was often better for the patient, but required more than two hands.

'Can you please hold the thoracoscope?' Connie asked him once they'd established clear visibility to the severely curved spine.

While Théo held the camera in place, Connie made another small incision between the ribs and passed a further scope inside the chest. The images from the camera were displayed real time onto monitors so the surgeons could accurately guide their instruments to the correct place. With the first few screws successfully placed into the misaligned vertebrae, suddenly the operative field became obscured by blood.

'Suction,' Connie said, quickly switching instruments.

'Let me,' Théo said, taking the suction from her. 'You get ready to cauterise the bleeder.' Théo held the thoracoscope steady in order to maintain visibility and directed the suction while Connie hurriedly manipulated the diathermy probe. It took some coordinated repositioning of the various instruments, but after a few tense moments of cooperation, anticipating what the other person might need, Connie successfully identified the bleeding capillary and quickly sealed it off.

Théo sighed with relief, seeing the same emotion in Connie's eyes as she briefly looked up at him.

'How are things looking there?' she asked the anaesthetist, who monitored Elodie's vital signs: pulse, blood pressure, respiration and blood oxygenation.

'Stable,' he confirmed.

Connie appeared to take a deep breath, carefully checking for further bleeding before she was happy to proceed. Then she looked down from the monitors, her eyes meeting Théo's.

'Thank you,' she said, curtly.

'No problem,' he replied, feeling as if he'd won a major victory not just a simple word of thanks. But as the operation resumed, time passing without further incident, Théo feared things between him and Connie as colleagues would be anything but straightforward. For one thing, he hadn't expected his attraction to her to be as intense as before. Not, it seemed, that he'd need to worry about there being a repeat of that night or starting relationship with a colleague. Connie was a focussed and intuitive surgeon, but, on a personal level, she obviously didn't like or trust him one bit.

St Raphaël Hospital was located in the medieval Latin Quarter of Paris, a short walk from the River Seine. Later that evening, Connie wrapped her woolly scarf around her neck as she left the hospital and crossed the road towards a cobbled square where one of the city's famous Christmas markets was in full swing. After a long day at work, Connie allowed herself to be lured by the magic. Twinkling lights were suspended overhead, strung from every building, lamp post and plane tree around the square. An ice-skating rink occupied the centre, encircled with numerous vendor stalls selling everything from Eiffel Tower Christmas decorations to *vin chaud* or mulled wine and every conceivable type of street food.

Desperately trying to block out Théo's unexpected and inconvenient appearance at St Raphaël, Connie mingled through the crowds of families and tourists, her mind stubbornly contemplating her first day of working with Théo.

After picking up her scalpel, she'd completely ignored their past and focussed on the case. To Connie's annoyance, Théo had seemed to anticipate her every move, instinctively clearing the operative field for better visibility and helpfully passing her instruments just when she needed them. He hadn't once tried to take over or dominate the operation, and by the time they'd sewn Elodie's wounds up, Connie had felt a begrudging gratitude that he'd been there, given his experience and the extra pair of hands. It was no surprise they were more able to effectively communicate about surgery than their personal issues. But rather than stay and chat after, she'd made some excuse and quickly left Theatre.

Now, Connie expelled a sigh. If he was going to be leading spinal surgery at St Raphaël, she would need to find some way to ignore him and all the memories he stirred. But with a possible pregnancy on which to focus, her obstinate attraction to a man from her past was the least of her concerns.

A young couple walking ahead of Connie stopped to kiss under a large, strategically placed bunch of mistletoe. Connie smiled, her heart thudding anew as she remembered the last man she'd kissed with that kind of passion had been Théo. Her handful of tame dates these past three years hadn't progressed beyond a chaste peck on the cheek. To her utter dismay, Théo was still infuriatingly sexy in the same way that had appealed to her the first time they'd met. Driven, intelligent and comfortable in his own skin, he had a way of looking at you as if you were the only person in the room.

Appalled that he could still affect her that way, that she still fancied him rotten, Connie ambled on through the market, which was crowded and lively with Christmas cheer. Surrounded by so many delicious cooking aromas, her stomach growled. After her long day of surgeries and the adrenaline of working with Théo, she was too tired to contemplate the idea of cooking when she arrived home. Instead, she headed for a stall selling hot *soupe à l'oignon* topped with crusty bread and melted Gruyère cheese. Hopefully the soup would still be warm by the time she arrived at her apartment, two *Métro* stops away.

'I had the same idea,' a deep voice at her side said.

Connie looked up to find Théo smiling broadly.

She was caught once more off guard by his stunning sex appeal, her pulse racing fast enough to leave her speechless. Wearing a smart woollen coat and a chic plaid scarf, his cheeks slightly ruddy from the cold, Théo looked ridiculously effortless Parisian chic. And despite the cool reception she'd given him that morning, he peered down at her with his signature confident smile and a glint of the heat it seemed impossible to ignore since they'd been intimate.

Connie smiled tightly, glancing away from that glint in his eyes. Her cheeks warmed with excitement even as she held herself rigid, annoyed by the physical attraction, which came so effortlessly.

'Lunch feels like a long time ago,' she muttered, watching the vendor spoon ladles of steaming soup into a takeaway container before sliding the cheese-topped toasted bread into a separate paper bag. Hoping to avoid the sexy scent of his cologne and the warmth from his body, she took a small step sideways.

'I agree. It does,' Théo said, placing some money on the counter for his own order. 'Can I buy you a *vin chaud*?' he asked Connie. 'To make up for my unexpected appearance this morning.'

Connie stiffened, shunted off balance by her body's violent responses to his smile and exhilarating eye contact. She didn't want to be rude, but nor could she handle any more of his distracting company. After all, she'd worked valiantly to avoid any mention of him these past three years while she'd put the hurt of that night behind her.

'No, thank you,' Connie replied primly, watching in horror as the stallholder packed both her and Théo's food into side-by-side bags as if they were one of the loved-up couples milling around the market, while another ladled Théo's mulled wine into a takeaway cup.

'Shame,' Théo said in the same playful tone after taking a sip. 'It's delicious.'

Connie pressed her lips together and looked away from his sexy mouth, disgusted with herself. Maybe if he hadn't been so supportive and instructive in Theatre, she might have found him easier to dismiss now. But they weren't friends. She had no intention of confiding her precious secret to him of all people—that she might be carrying his brother's baby.

'Well, I'm heading home,' Connie said, scooping up her dinner and offering Théo a polite smile. 'Goodnight.'

She turned away. Better he understood that she had no personal interest in him whatsoever. She had no interest in any man, especially not one who'd essentially kicked her when she was down. It had taken months after discovering Guy's horrible deception for Connie to even face socialising. Then, when she'd finally accepted one of Tris's many invitations, to his brother's Christmas *réveillon*, she'd foolishly slept with Théo and lived to regret it. She should have known her judgement had still been flawed. But trusting Guy, who she'd believed to be the one, only to find out he'd been living a lie, had left her riddled with self-doubt.

'Hold on.' Théo strode after her, easily catching up. 'Are you heading for the *Métro*?'

'Yes.' Without breaking her stride—no easy feat given the slowly ambling crowds—she tried to put some distance between her and Théo.

'Me too,' he said, still on her tail. 'I'll walk with you.'

Connie paused to shoot him a horrified look. 'Haven't we spent long enough in each other's company today? Why can't you simply ignore me the way we've been ignoring each other for the past three years?'

Bad enough that she'd been forced to set aside how he'd hurt her and watch him work today, to witness how impressive a surgeon he was. Meticulous and diligent and clearly dedicated to his career. There'd been no sign of that arrogance she'd detected when she'd overheard him tell Tris that by sleeping with her he'd been on the rebound and made a mistake.

'I hoped we could talk,' he said, reasonably, 'away from work.' Distracted by a couple of excited children tottering towards the ice rink on their skates, he smiled down at them then glanced back at Connie.

Connie shuddered as her hormones surged. Why did he have to be so good at everything? So sexy and likeable and charming? But his façade couldn't be trusted and she'd been a fool to think he'd be any different from her ex, Guy. After all, they'd been engaged and living together. After four years together, she'd made plans for a future—marriage, a family—that Guy had rewritten with someone else. He'd deceived her and had a child with another woman. She'd felt stupid that she hadn't seen through him. Of course, he'd taken advantage of the fact her career often involved long and unpredictable hours in order to conduct his affair.

'I was actually hoping to invite you out for a drink some time,' Théo went on, smiling, unaware that Connie felt suddenly nauseous with humiliation and rejection. 'After all, we're hardly strangers. And it's Christmas.'

'I thought we said everything we needed to this morning,' she threw out dismissively, heading for the nearest exit from the square, desperate to get away from him and the inconvenient memories he stirred up, both the thrill of that night in his bed and her raw vulnerability when the hurt Guy had caused came rushing back the next morning.

And go for a drink…? Was he serious? She was doing her best to forget that he'd come back into her life, today of all days. All she really wanted to do was go home and dream about her optimistic future and motherhood and the life that might, right now, be growing inside her.

'I have questions,' he said, stepping aside for a pregnant woman pushing a toddler in a buggy.

'About work?' she asked, pausing at the exit. Maybe if she answered his query quickly, he'd leave her alone.

'No,' he said as they fell into step once more. 'About what you said in Theatre, about honesty and transparency. I know you have trust issues when it comes to relationships...' he added quietly.

Connie winced. That night, she'd told him she'd recently gone through a bad break-up. Likewise, Théo had confided in her about his mutual-consent divorce, something Tris had mentioned in passing. She'd found their similar experiences comforting, foolishly assuming they had more in common than their careers and Tris. But soon realised she didn't know this man.

'But have I done something to offend you,' he went on, 'aside from taking the job at St Raphaël, that is?' His good-natured smile and his enquiry left her itching with frustration.

'Really,' Connie said, her stomach twisting with discomfort. 'You want to do this here? Now?'

She glanced pointedly at the cheerful crowds milling around them. The last thing she wanted was to relive that humiliating morning when, for a moment after waking up, she'd felt desirable again after Guy's betrayal and hopeful that she might be ready to move on.

'Do what?' He frowned, as if he had no idea what he'd said that morning. 'I'm trying to clear the air, Connie. We have Tris and Victor's wedding coming up soon and we have to work together, after all.'

'That's down to you,' Connie muttered, wishing she'd confronted him three years ago rather than sneaking out of his apartment with her tail between her legs. But she'd still been wounded from the way hateful Guy had decimated her confidence with his deception and cruelty. She hadn't been able to face another confrontation back then. But she was harder now. Less gullible.

A steely glint entered his stare. 'You're right. I made a judgement call based on a career-topping job,' Théo said with a sigh. 'I assumed that you and I could work out what went wrong three years ago and be civil. But if I've done something to upset you, tell me and I'll apologise. Besides,' he added, stepping closer and lowering his head, his stare dipping to her mouth and inconveniently heating her blood, 'I've only ignored you because I thought that was what *you* wanted. You're the one who sneaked out without a word that Christmas.'

She stepped closer too, the fact that she still found him wildly attractive fuelling her indignation. 'Are you saying you wanted me to stay

for breakfast? Because that wasn't the impression you gave.'

His frown deepened. 'You never gave me a
chance to say anything. You just left and then
ignored my texts.'

Connie inhaled a deep breath, the humiliation
extinguishing the sparks being this close to him
ignited. 'I heard you, Théo. Heard you telling
Tristan that we'd slept together and how much
you regretted it. *That's* why I left that morning.
I'd heard enough to realise that what I thought
we'd shared didn't mean anything to you.'

Wishing she could stalk off as fast as her slosh-
ing soup and comfy boots could carry her, she
paused at the flicker of shame and hesitation in
his eyes.

'I'm sorry,' he said quietly, his strong brow dipping in a frown. 'Obviously I didn't know that
you'd overheard our conversation. But that's not
true.' He stepped closer and dropped his voice
further. 'It did mean something, Connie. Did you
tell Tris you'd overheard?'

His voice was full of apology, but Connie
shook the knowledge of his regret from her head.
It would be easier to work with him and ignore
their chemistry if she clung to her dislike and
distrust. This was exactly why she preferred to
be alone. Even now, three and a half years since
she'd discovered Guy's deception after overhear-

ing him on the phone to his lover, she still had to maintain her guard against the pain.

'No. I told him you and I wouldn't be happening again,' she said, raising her chin. 'That the subject was closed.'

She glanced across the street longingly. The *Métro* station and escape were just in sight.

'Obviously it's not closed,' he said reasonably, his voice that same low murmur that had groaned sexy things that night, 'if you're still upset with me.'

'I'm not upset. I told you, for me the sex was instantly forgettable.' Connie kept her voice calm as she lied. 'I only left without confronting you that morning because I was angry. You acted as if I expected some grand commitment from you, which was ridiculous.' Of course, he'd acted so carefree and unemotional that night she'd assumed he was well and truly over his marriage and ready to move on. A part of her had even wondered if that night might have been the start of something between them, more fool her.

'We had ill-judged sex that we both regretted after too much wine at a Christmas party,' she continued, trying to conceal how hurt she'd been to hear him dismiss what for her had been an amazing night. 'But you told your brother, my best friend, that you didn't want to see me again. What makes you so certain that I would have wanted to see *you* again?' She pointed her finger at the centre of his chest, finally losing the threads of her composure.

A few of the people enjoying the market cast them amused looks as if they were in the middle of a lovers' tiff. When one man glanced pointedly at Théo and then raised his gaze skywards, Connie, too, looked up.

Théo and she stood underneath an archway strung with twinkling lights from which was suspended another large bunch of mistletoe tied with a red velvet ribbon.

Connie's cheeks flamed with embarrassment. Only Théo could make her argue in a public place with an audience. She met his stare once more, furious. But further admonishment was trapped in her throat by the seductive look in his eyes and the answering shudder it sent through her body. Infuriatingly, in spite of everything, she still fancied him.

'Shame to pass up on an opportunity,' Théo said, a suggestive smile tugging at his lips. He tilted his head cheekily and raised one eyebrow as if in invitation, obviously suggesting they simply kiss and make up.

'You have got to be kidding me?' Connie scoffed and spluttered, her pulse racing at the memory of that last time they'd locked lips and the speed at which that late-night Christmas kiss had escalated to a night of intense and unforgettable passion. Théo was an amazing kisser. But did he really think he could kiss his way into her good books after his past indiscretion and gate-crashing her surgery?

He shrugged. 'When I knew I was definitely joining St Raphaël, I was curious to see if our chemistry was still alive.' His dark eyes bored into hers. 'Now I know that it is.'

'It's also irrelevant,' Connie said, impressed with the coolness of her voice given the way her entire body seemed about to melt. 'I don't trust you and I'm happily single. I've moved on.' To the next chapter in her life. Having the child she'd always wanted. Taking life into her own hands and abandoning the search for love and commitment from untrustworthy men. 'I'm sorry for you if you haven't,' she finished, an annoying niggle of compassion for him blooming in her chest.

Now she understood that when they'd hooked up, she too had been on the rebound. Vulnerable and needy. She'd slept with Théo that night partly to prove she could still be attractive to the opposite sex, despite Guy's cheating. But she refused to feel ashamed for that, especially when Théo had clearly had his own agenda that night.

'And I'm sorry for being indiscreet that morning. You're absolutely right. I should have spoken to you first, not Tris,' he said, regret wiping the flirtatious smile from his face.

Regret that they were arguing in public or that she'd turned down the opportunity of a kiss?

'Tris and I are very close. I admitted to him that I shouldn't have seduced you because I probably wasn't ready to move on, which wasn't fair to you. My divorce made me feel like a failure and the night we met I was still a bit of a mess…'

'Maybe I seduced you,' she interrupted, deaf to his explanations because all day she'd been telling herself it was easier to lump him in with her devious, self-serving ex as just another man she couldn't trust. 'Maybe I was on the rebound, too,' she said defensively.

He stepped closer and dropped his voice, his glittering stare turning darkly intense. 'I think we seduced each other, Connie.' His gaze skittered over her mouth as if he desperately wanted that kiss. As if he saw through her bravado. Saw how much she still fancied him and how hard she was trying to forget.

Connie's pulse throbbed in her fingertips, danger signs flashing in her head. He was right about chemistry. She had no idea who'd touched who that night, but with the first touch they'd burst into flames as if doused in petrol. Even now, her entire body flushed hot from delicious memories. 'It makes no difference now.' She dragged in a frigid breath, her insides trembling with adrenaline and the need to get away from him. 'You've apologised for talking about me behind my back with my best friend, making out I wanted a ring after one night. After misguidedly trusting my cheating ex, I should have known better. It was a mistake we both regret. Let's just leave it there.'

She tried to step away but the flash of anger in his stare stalled her departure.

'Hold on,' he said, inching closer so Connie grew more aware of his imposing height, strong build and broad-chested manliness, which only reminded her of how it had felt to be in his arms. 'I might have expressed doubts that I was ready for more than one night to my brother, something I'd planned to say to you when you woke that morning, by the way, but that's the extent of my wrongdoing. I'm no cheat, Connie. My marriage ended for other reasons. Mutual reasons. And I'd been divorced three months the night we met. I think you're overreacting here. Transferring your anger at the man who hurt you onto me. Maybe I shouldn't have slept with you that night. I regret the timing, but I don't for one second regret what happened between us.'

Connie spluttered, confused by his openness and far more excited than she should be by his sexy admission.

'Well, I do,' she lied, still clinging to her indignation. She would never know if she still would have regretted sleeping with him if she hadn't overheard his conversation that morning. But she hated the idea that she'd been so vulnerable and easily hurt so soon after Guy.

Desperate to flee the way Théo was making her question certainties—that he couldn't be trusted, that she didn't need sex, that she was done with relationships—she fisted her hand on her hip. 'I understand that we have to work together, and I'm glad we've finally cleared the air. But unless we're collaborating on a patient, there really is nothing more to say.'

She was going to have a baby. Another man's baby. Even if she could forgive Théo, even if she wanted another night of mindless passion with him, she now had other priorities.

'Okay,' he said quietly and stepped back, a determined mask falling over his expression. 'If that's how you want to leave things.'

'It is,' Connie said, her adrenaline draining to leave a vague sense of what felt like disappointment. But that was silly and probably just a re-action to her fatigue, to all the Christmas cheer around them, to having finally had the confron-tation she'd put off for three years while she'd re-covered her decimated self-esteem.

With her pulse bounding and her throat ach-ing, as if she were close to tears, she stepped away from him and offered a tight smile. 'Enjoy your soup.'

Then she crossed the road and ducked into the

Métro station and headed for her train, replaying every word of their conversation over and over until nothing made sense, least of all the confusing swirl of her emotions.

CHAPTER THREE

STILL RELIVING HIS frustrating interaction with Connie the night before, Théo arrived at the hospital from his early morning session at the gym determined to do as she'd asked and ignore every infuriating, gorgeous inch of her. It certainly wasn't how he'd imagined their reunion would play out. Secretly, part of him had hoped that if they'd successfully cleared the air that spark might still be there, which of course it was. Only more of a raging inferno than a spark.

But if she could ignore the obvious chemistry between them, he would too. Because Connie was the kind of distraction he in no way needed. His life was finally in a good place. Both he and Tris had fulfilling careers they loved. His brother was about to be married, having found the love of his life in Victor. And Théo had spent most of his adult life convinced that if Tris was happy, he could be too.

Not to mention it was Christmas soon. Théo's favourite time of year: a precious time to be with friends and loved ones and make family memories. And, of course, he looked forward to his annual Christmas *réveillon*.

He'd just sat at his desk to check his work emails when his younger brother appeared in the doorway.

'Very nice,' Tris said, about Théo's office, which was small, but had a view of the Seine from the window. 'Settling in all right?'

'Come in and close the door,' Théo said, standing to briefly embrace Tris, who worked as a renal physician at St Raphaël and had been in Connie's year at medical school, which was where they'd become firm friends.

'What's up?' Tris asked, taking a seat and resting one ankle on the opposite knee.

'I was hoping you might help me answer that question,' Théo replied, observing Tris, who appeared a little distracted. Perhaps, like Théo, he had a busy day ahead.

'Oh? In what way? You're being very cryptic,' his brother pointed out with a mocking smile.

Théo dragged in a breath and exhaled. 'It's about Connie. I spoke to her yesterday.' And it had cost him dearly: a restless night of erotic dreams and waking fantasies where, instead of dismissing his apology, she forgave him and they'd utilised that convenient bunch of mistletoe.

Tris winced. 'I tried to warn her about you

yesterday. Maybe if you'd allowed me to tell her sooner...'

'I thought I was doing the right thing,' Théo said. 'There seemed no point upsetting her until it was confirmed and I'd actually signed the contract. And I didn't know they'd want me to start right away or that she'd booked time off.'

'Still, you knew your paths would cross,' Tris said, brushing a speck of lint from his immaculate trousers and avoiding Théo's stare.

'Of course,' Théo said, seeking patience. 'We work in the same speciality and now the same department. I hoped we could clear the air and move on. What I didn't expect was that she'd still be upset with me over something that happened three years ago. I...hurt her. Did you know about that?' Of course, he'd been horrified that she'd overheard that conversation, but he was genuinely sorry.

Tristan shook his head, clearly clueless. 'Know about what?' he asked, frowning warily. 'What did you do?' As a loyal friend, Tris rarely talked to Théo about Connie.

Théo sighed, certain there would be more sleepless nights thinking about her in his future. 'Did you know that she overheard us talking the morning after the Christmas party where she and I...met?' Met? Insert *had a night of wild sex*.

'Of course not,' Tris said, appearing genuinely

shocked. 'She never said a word to me but that explains a lot.'

'What *did* she say?' Théo pushed, still embarrassed that he'd been so indiscreet. He'd awoken before dawn, left her asleep in his bed, gone to make coffee and found Tris in the kitchen doing the same. The minute Tris had seen the two cups of coffee and guessed that he'd slept with Connie, he'd reeled off a string of warnings about how badly she'd been hurt by her ex. Théo had reassured Tris that he wasn't ready for more than casual sex anyway, unaware that Connie had overheard him express regret for the timing.

Tris shrugged. 'She didn't really want to talk about you at all. I assumed she'd had an…underwhelming night.'

Théo scoffed and tilted his head. 'She had a great night, trust me.' They'd had sex three times. He'd dragged orgasm after orgasm from her. They'd acted like insatiable teenagers.

Tris held up his hands. 'Okay, I believe you. But I didn't want the details. She's my friend and you're my brother.' He gave a small shudder. 'Anyway, when I asked her why she left without telling me she said she was embarrassed that she'd slept with you and asked if we could never talk about it again. I'm a good friend, so I agreed. I assumed it was bad timing for her given what Guy had put her through. He really hurt her. She hadn't recovered enough to start dating, which was why I was so surprised to learn the two of you had…hit it off. After you'd confided in me that you weren't ready for anything serious either, I thought the subject was closed and we could all move on, no harm done.'

'Except there was harm done.' Théo impatiently tapped at the desk with his index finger as he recalled Connie's hurt expression from the night before and the wash of shame he'd felt. 'I obviously hurt her, because she hates my guts now, which is very inconvenient because I actually like and respect her as a colleague and we have to work together.' Not to mention she was still as sexy as sin… Another thing he'd need to ignore.

'Do you want me to talk to her and explain?' Tris asked, looking a little uncomfortable at the prospect of doing Théo's dirty work. 'I need to apologise to her anyway. I should have warned her sooner that you might be joining the team.'

'No, I'll clean up my own mess,' he said. 'I just wondered if you had any extra insights, that's all.'

Tris shook his head thoughtfully. 'I took her at her word. Assumed she regretted sleeping with you.'

Théo pressed his lips together in frustration. 'Oh, she regrets it all right… But I take full responsibility.' Because hot on the heels of her ex, Théo too had let Connie down and inadvertently hurt her. Maybe Anaïs, his ex-wife, was right.

Maybe he was too emotionally distant. Marriage between him and Anaïs had been fine for a couple of years when they'd seemed to want the same things. But she'd kept putting off the family they'd discussed, blaming him for the something that was missing from their relationship and stating a baby wouldn't fix it. So when she'd announced, after that final row, it was over, he'd felt devastating guilt along with a depressing sense of inevitability.

'Don't worry,' he reassured Tris, who wore a concerned frown. 'I'll sort things out with Connie.'

He would apologise again and move on because, since his divorce, Théo avoided complicated in favour of casual. In his experience, relationships weren't worth all the heartache and loss. So what if his family consisted only of him, Tris and Tris's partner, Victor? Quality was better than quantity any day.

'Why did you come to see me anyway?' he asked Tris, shoving Connie from his mind once more.

Tris winced, glancing away. 'I um… I have something to tell you. Funny story, in fact, because it also involves Connie.'

'Okay…' He stiffened. 'Let's hear it, then.'

'Well,' Tris began hesitantly, 'you know that Victor and I definitely don't want children, right?'

Théo nodded and Tris went on. 'I mean, we

knew that when we met and neither of us is likely to change our mind.'

'Okay...' Théo nodded, aware that he needed to be on the ward in five minutes to review Elodie Verdier. If Tris didn't get to the point soon, they'd have to reschedule this conversation.

'Well, Connie's always wanted a family,' Tris explained, growing cagier, 'and she's given up on finding Mr Right. She has understandable trust issues when it comes to dating, so she decided to go it alone and I um...'

Braced for bad news, Théo shook his head, interrupting. 'Please don't tell me what I think you're going to tell me.'

Tris shrugged, his cheeks flushing. 'I just wanted you to know. Victor agreed and Connie and I discussed all the pros and cons. I said I'd be her sperm donor.'

Théo stared in shock as if he'd been punched. One, Connie had given up on men at the age of thirty-five? Two, just because Tris and Victor were about to become happily married didn't mean there wouldn't be emotional implications if Tris was to father a child. And three, what right did Théo have to utter one single word of caution when he himself, years before as a cash-strapped medical student, had donated his sperm to one of the city's fertility clinics?

'This way,' Tris continued, unaware of Théo's turmoil, 'she has the child she wants and I'll always be there as Uncle Tris because of our friendship. I guess that will make you Uncle Théo.' He laughed nervously, but Théo couldn't join in.

Uncle Théo? He closed his eyes and sighed under his breath. Growing up without a father, and ever since their mother and then grandmother died and they'd been placed into foster care aged twelve and nine, Théo had been looking out for Tristan. As an adult, he'd desperately tried to be a male role model for his brother and to recreate the family stability they'd missed out on as boys. He was proud of the kind, intelligent man his brother had become. It warmed Théo to know that, while their family had been snatched away from them and while his own marriage had failed, Tris was in a loving and committed relationship.

But a sperm donor…? Connie potentially having Théo's niece or nephew. When she could hardly stand him. When he knew exactly what it was like to grow up thinking your father didn't love you enough to stick around.

'Are you sure this is a good idea after everything we've been through?' Théo asked cautiously. 'Even if you won't be raising it, a baby is a serious emotional consideration. We know from our upbringing that family is everything. A child needs to know both its parents, to know it's loved. And aside from that, my main concern is that you'll somehow be hurt.'

Could Tris really be in Connie's life, see his biological child all the time and not yearn for more contact? Théo wouldn't be able to be an absent father. And what if Tris and Connie's friendship broke down? What then? Would he and Tris lose another family member they loved?

Tris shook his head, adamant. 'Connie is my best friend. We're always going to be a part of each other's lives anyway, and she was heartbroken when Guy cheated and got the other woman pregnant.'

Théo gaped, stunned by this new detail and horrified for Connie. 'I know…' he said, his mind whirring through all the potential pitfalls for his brother. 'But there are clinics. She could have a child with an anonymous donor. Hell, some crazy people buy sperm on the Internet. Just think about it,' he urged. 'A child is a big commitment, even if you won't be raising it. And what happens if you sign away your parental rights and one day Connie denies you access to your child?'

Tris's expression turned guilty. 'Thanks for the words of warning. I know you're always looking out for me, and I appreciate how much you care. But it's kind of too late for the pep talk. Connie underwent the procedure earlier this week. She could already be pregnant for all we know.'

'What? Are you serious?' Théo's blood drained from his body, head to toe. Was Connie already carrying his brother's baby? What would that mean for her and Théo's relationship? Not that there was going to be a relationship beyond a professional one, but their chemistry didn't seem to care. And what about this innocent baby that might grow up desperate for its father's love?

'Yes,' Tris said. 'That's why I'm coming to you now. I thought you should know that Connie might be having your niece or nephew. And I'm happy to hand over my parental rights, otherwise I'd never have offered.'

'Which is why you maybe should have come to me sooner so we could discuss this,' Théo gritted out in frustration, his past colliding with the present. He himself had always wanted a family, which was why it had been so devastating that Anaïs had changed her mind about having a family with him.

But just because Tris felt comfortable fathering Connie's child, didn't mean that Théo would feel comfortable having a niece or nephew he never saw. He'd spent most of his life craving the perfect family. Would he be able to ignore a child he was related to just because Connie had given up on men and found a way to have a baby alone? But given her dislike of him, Connie was unlikely to allow him to have any contact with the child, anyway. He'd be in a horrible position with no rights…

Just then Tris's pager sounded and he stood, silencing it. 'Sorry, I need to go. My clinic is about to begin.'

Théo reeled. Talk about dropping a bomb-shell…

'Wait,' he said as Tris headed for the door. 'Does Connie know that you planned to tell me?' He didn't want any further misunderstandings between them, not when he somehow needed to wriggle his way back into her good books for multiple reasons.

'She gave me permission to tell whoever I saw fit,' Tris said. 'It's in the contract we had drawn up.'

'How very efficient of you both,' Théo muttered darkly, not sure if he wanted to hug or berate his brother. But neither was necessary. Tris wasn't a child. If he and Connie thought this was a sensible plan, who was Théo to argue? Only losing their caregivers at a young age, growing up without a proper family, had made Théo determined to give Tris as close to a traditional family as he could manage. This foolproof plan of theirs made him very nervous indeed.

'When you see her,' Tris said, hesitating in the doorway, 'just go easy on her, yeah?'

'Me go easy on *her*?' Théo laughed, recalling his hostile reception from Connie the day before and the dressing-down she'd given him under the mistletoe.

'She's been pretty hormonal lately, what with the ovulation shots, and I guess it's only going to get worse if the procedure worked and she is pregnant.' Tris shrugged. 'I don't know. Just be nice.'

Be nice? Théo sighed. He could try, but then Connie had made it clear she wanted absolutely nothing from him. He didn't think him playing *nice* would make one bit of difference.

CHAPTER FOUR

LATER THAT AFTERNOON, after successfully avoiding Théo all day, Connie took an urgent call from the neurology registrar, who had a patient in A & E for her to review.

'I'll be right there,' she said, hanging up the phone.

She left her office and rushed to the emergency department, her mind snagged, as it had been for most of the past twenty-four hours since he'd joined the team at St Raphaël, on Théo.

As she'd feared, he'd dominated her thoughts for most of the previous evening after their confrontation. She'd been forced to admit that when he'd accused her of taking out her Guy-directed hurt and anger on him, he might have had a point. When she'd closed her eyes for sleep, all she could see were his regrets and that sexy seductive look in his eyes as they'd stood underneath the mistletoe at the Christmas market. All she'd heard over the hum of the city noise outside, which normally lulled her into unconsciousness, was him admitting that their chemistry was still alive.

On reviewing the conversation she'd overheard three years ago in light of Théo's explanation, Connie found there'd been a ring of truth to his apologies. The night she'd slept with him, she'd assumed he was moving on after his divorce because he hadn't seemed cut up. But she more than anyone knew how the effects of a bad break-up could be long lasting.

Maybe that night had simply been bad timing for both him and Connie.

But his shocking revelations changed nothing. She was focussed on becoming a mother and didn't need a man. Her trust had, she suspected, been irreparably damaged by Guy's deceit. She never wanted to feel that vulnerable again. It just wasn't worth the risk. Not even if it meant going without sex as hot as she'd shared with Théo.

Feeling a momentary twinge of regret, she sighed as she entered the emergency department wondering if taking Théo at his word made her a trusting fool. It certainly didn't help her to dismiss and ignore him…

Glad to have work on which to focus, Connie marched up to the neuro registrar, who stood at a computer terminal looking harassed. Before Connie could take a look at the notes or hear the other doctor's history of the patient, she spied Théo striding their way, his handsome face wearing a frown of concern.

'What do we have?' he asked as he joined them, flicking Connie an inscrutable look that made her rapid pulse surge faster.

'Fifty-four-year-old male with lower back pain,' the registrar said, addressing them both. 'He gives a classic history of cauda equina syndrome—bladder dysfunction in the form of urinary retention, pain radiating down the back of his legs, numbness of the buttocks and weakness of both feet.'

'Any history of trauma?' Connie asked, glancing at Théo to see from his expression that he shared Connie's clinical concern for the patient. Cauda equina syndrome was a rare but serious spinal emergency usually caused by a herniated lumbar disc.

'None,' the registrar said.

'When did the symptoms begin?' Théo asked the very question that Connie was thinking, proving how professionally attuned they were.

'Yesterday,' the registrar said. 'He thought it was sciatica and would resolve, but the symptoms are worsening.'

'So we're against the clock,' Connie confirmed, catching Théo's eye. They both knew that if left untreated the nerve compression could lead to permanent leg paralysis, bladder and bowel issues and sexual dysfunction. Which was why the emergency treatment of choice was a surgical decompression of the ruptured disc.

'The MRI results should be back now,' the registrar said, logging into the computer. She opened the radiology report and all three of them scanned the results and the relevant scan images and X-rays.

'There, between L4 and L5,' Théo said, pointing out the obvious disc herniation between the lowest two lumbar vertebrae.

'Thanks.' Connie reached for the notes the registrar had taken. 'Dr Augustin and I will examine him and consent him for an emergency microdiscectomy. If you could make sure he's ready for a general anaesthetic with all relevant blood work and call the anaesthetist.'

While the neurology registrar rushed off to organise blood tests, Connie scanned the patient's medical history before passing the tablet to Théo.

'Do you want me to take this case?' she asked, uncertain of him after their talk the night before and the way she'd behaved so defensively. But they were each professional enough to set aside their personal issues and focus on work.

'I'm still getting used to the theatre protocols here,' he said, wearing a small frown of concern. 'So if you can tolerate my presence, I'd welcome the opportunity to assist.'

'Of course.' Connie nodded, her concern for

the patient outweighing the need to keep Théo and his insistent attractiveness at arm's length.

She might be having his brother's baby. There was no space in her life for romance, flirtation or casual sex, least of all with Théo.

'I like to try the endoscopic approach first,' he said, glancing her way as if seeking her opinion on the best course of action in this case.

'Even with herniations of this size?' she asked, surprised. 'My first inclination was a tubular microdiscectomy.' The procedure she favoured was slightly more invasive for the patient, but visibility was improved, leading to shorter duration under anaesthetic.

'Why don't we examine him, review the scans again and then decide?' Théo diplomatically suggested, clearly trying to make amends for the past and his first day.

Connie nodded, unable to argue with his reasonable suggestion. 'Sounds like a plan,' she said, heading off to find the patient, aware of Théo behind as if the air between them were electrically charged.

For the time being, it seemed there would be little escape from his distracting presence, from the sexy memories, or the way, despite it all, working with him was easy. All she could hope for was that her hormones would soon tire of constantly lusting after him and give up the ghost. And if that failed, she'd simply wait it out until she became too heavily pregnant to do anything about their chemistry. Easy.

After the emergency micro-endoscopic discectomy on their cauda equina syndrome patient, Théo was just about to leave the hospital for the night when he spied Connie emerging from the theatre changing rooms up ahead.

He hesitated, his heart pounding with trepidation and the ever-present flicker of excitement the sight of her induced. Connie was the sort of woman who appealed to him on every level. Whether she was dressed in scrubs or the smartest suit, her glossy brown hair tied up and tamed, she always looked elegant and sophisticated and yet feminine. Smart, driven and with a strength of character he couldn't help but admire. He found her company both addictive and intriguing.

Of course, now that she might be pregnant with his niece or nephew, there were bigger fish to fry than their attraction. Tris's news about being her donor had left him unsettled, probably because he had no memories of his own father, who'd left when Théo was two and before Tris was born. If Théo and Connie were going to be a permanent fixture in each other's lives, connected by her and Tris's child, they should at least try to get along. For Tris's sake and for the sake of the child. Who knew, maybe the pregnancy and the family connection would kill their chemistry for good? He could only hope that would be the case, because nothing else seemed to be working.

'Connie,' he called out, torn between ignoring her as promised, and keeping his word to Tris by playing nice. But loyalty to his brother won. Théo didn't want bad blood between him and Connie to sour things for Tris's relationship with his child. Not when the situation they'd engineered between them was already so unconventional.

Connie turned, pulling on her coat. 'I'm heading home,' she said, eyeing him warily but less frostily than before. Was she thawing towards him now that he'd had a chance to apologise for his slip-up three years ago?

'I won't hold you up.' He caught up to her, catching the scent of her perfume and concealing a wince. That floral scent was so distracting. She'd left it on his sheets and pillow three years ago and his body remembered, his blood pumping harder. 'I just wanted you to know that Tristan confided in me about your um…arrangement.'

'Oh.' She quickly recovered from her surprise and tilted up her chin, her guard obviously rising as if she expected Théo's disapproval. 'And?'

'And nothing,' he said, swallowing down most of his reservations for fear of causing offence. 'I'm simply being transparent, as requested. I'm sure the two of you know what you're doing. It's no one else's business, mine included.'

'I agree,' she said, and rolled her gorgeous amber-flecked eyes. 'But I sense a but all the same.'

Théo took her mocking smile as a win. At least she wasn't stomping off angrily. But he had so many buts he didn't know where to begin.

'Obviously,' he said, quietly, emotion tightening his throat, 'I have concerns for Tris. I'm protective of my brother. I'd be letting him down if I wasn't uneasy that he might somehow have future regrets if there is a baby. Tris never knew our father and I don't really have any memories of him either.' He swallowed, the deeply ingrained feelings of loss and rejection stinging like a reopened wound. 'Tris has a big heart, which can leave him exposed to being hurt.'

'He's also a grown man capable of making his own decisions,' she countered, but a small frown tightened her lips, as if Tris had never really talked about their father, which was unsurprising to Théo.

He shrugged. 'I know. But after losing our mother and then our grandmother when we were boys, and growing up in care, you can understand how family means a lot to us.' Obviously more so to Théo than Tris. With the exception of that desperate sperm donation in his early twenties, Théo could never do what Tris had signed up for. He couldn't live knowing he'd fathered a child with someone he knew. A child he might see but not help to raise, or, if the worst happened, a child he loved but, because of circumstances, rarely saw. He'd never understood how his own father could make two sons and just walk away without ever reaching out. He and Tris had talked about it over the years and neither of them was interested in finding or knowing the man. It was enough that they had each other and the memories of the years they'd spent with their two maternal figures.

'I'm just concerned that when the baby arrives,' he continued, 'Tris might regret signing away his parental rights.' He allowed his voice to harden slightly. 'I don't want him to be hurt or lose any more family than he already has.'

As if it were *his* hypothetical baby they were discussing, Théo's throat turned dry with fear. In Théo's experience, people who should have cared for him disappeared and people he loved and cared about tended to be snatched away. He just wanted to protect Tris, and even his and Connie's child, from more heartache. All kids deserved to know both their parents.

Connie swallowed, her expression turning serious and a little guilty. 'I don't want him to be hurt either. He's my best friend. I care about him as much as you.'

She blinked up at him and, for the first time since they'd come back into each other's lives, Théo saw the unguarded Connie. His heart lurched with compassion. She'd been badly hurt too.

'I know you do.' He tried to smile, but his protective urges wouldn't be silenced. A part of him still felt uncomfortable by Tris and Connie's clinical arrangement, despite their reassurances. 'It heartens me that you care about Tris's feelings. I guess not wanting him to be hurt is the one thing on which you and I can agree.'

Connie gave him a small nod, assessing him with those big brown eyes. For a second, it was as if they were back in his kitchen, moments before they kissed. That unfathomable connection between them powerful.

'I'd never stop Tris seeing the baby if that's what he wanted,' she said, quietly, as if she felt the electricity too and was scared to move.

'I'm not suggesting you would,' Théo said, concealing a sigh because the effect she had on him was beyond irrelevant. 'But you must agree your arrangement has the potential to create…emotional complications.'

Flushing slightly, she raised her chin. 'I think Tris and I have it under control.' She buttoned up her coat, clearly preparing to walk away. 'But thanks for letting me know that he's confided in you. Now I don't need to worry about keeping it a secret.'

Because he wasn't wholly comforted, and, maybe because he wasn't ready for her to walk away, Théo stepped closer and dropped his voice. 'Listen, I think you and I should try to get along, don't you? I know we got off to a bad start yesterday. I know I behaved indiscreetly three years ago. But I've sincerely apologised, and, if we take our sexual chemistry off the table, surely we can get along for Tris's sake. Especially if there is a baby.'

As if she was made uncomfortable by his closeness and his mention of their attraction, her pupils dilated, her cheeks flushed and her breaths gusted excitedly. But she didn't move away or even argue the presence of their chemistry.

'It's Tris and Victor's wedding soon,' Théo went on, pushing his rationale. 'I'm best man and you're maid of honour. And if you're having my brother's baby, we're about to become family.'

'I wouldn't say that,' she said, her wariness back.

Clearly it would take a lot for him to win back her trust.

'One of the most attractive things about having a child this way,' she said, 'is that the baby will be *all* mine. I'm happy doing this alone. I don't need anyone else.'

Théo nodded placatingly even as his skin began to crawl. Depressingly, uncles had no legal parental rights. 'But technically,' he said, needing to defend both his and Tris's agenda all the same, 'I'll be the baby's uncle. That's important to me, Connie. Family is important, don't you think?'

'I guess. Sometimes...' She shrugged, clearly dubious about allowing Théo into her circle of trust. 'Sometimes family can be overwhelming, noisy and opinionated. My brothers drive me mad whenever we're all together. Most families aren't perfect.'

Théo tilted his head in challenge. 'I'm afraid I wouldn't really know. My family is Tris. Look,' he said, inhaling a deep breath for patience, 'I'm having my annual Christmas Eve party in Provence this year. It will be a small gathering—Tris, Victor and some close friends—and I'd love for you to be there, too, as would Tris, I'm sure.'

'Provence?' she asked, her eyebrows raised in curiosity as her stare shifted over his face.

Théo shrugged, equally curious about how she normally spent Christmas. 'I inherited a home there a few years ago, from an old professor who mentored me at medical school.'

'Wow. Impressive,' she muttered and glanced at her feet, her cheeks colouring.

Was she, like him, remembering the previous Christmas party she'd attended, the night they'd spent together, barely sleeping, having sex over and over until they were both exhausted?

While his pulse surged, he inched closer and dropped his voice, hoping humour might win her over. 'I promise not to seduce you this time.'

'Very funny.' She laughed ironically then snagged her bottom lip with her teeth as she looked up at him with something akin to uncertainty.

'You don't have to decide now,' he said, sensing her imminent refusal. 'I just thought, as we work together and we both love Tris and if you have his baby, that will make us all family, you and I should try to put the past behind us and get along.'

Aware of his emotional manipulation tactics, she narrowed her eyes. 'I don't really do big family parties, especially at Christmas,' she said, that thread of steel in her voice. 'In fact, I usually work over the holidays. In my experience Christmas is an excuse for people to drink too much and behave badly.'

Was she talking about them sleeping together again? Beating him over the head with her regrets, which, he was aware, she hadn't recanted in light of his explanation and apology?

'My siblings all have children,' she added with a sigh, 'so it's always noisy chaos. My uncles, aunts and cousins congregate at my parents' house. There are usually at least two family members who have a disagreement and fall out. I prefer to avoid all the drama.'

'That doesn't sound very festive of you,' he teased with a smile. 'Where's your Christmas spirit? I always make the most of family moments, even if it's just for me and Tris and now Victor. And if your plan works, next year you'll have a child of your own.'

Théo's heart thumped harder, the urge to win just a sliver of her trust a personal challenge.

Now that Tris had volunteered to father Connie's child, it seemed more important than ever before to make the most of family get-togethers. So that Connie and Tris's baby knew its father's side of the family. Tris might be happy to have a casual relationship with Connie's child, but Théo would want to be a close uncle. To be there for anything the kid might need. To shower it with love and attention and gifts so it grew up in no doubt it was safe, loved and accepted.

'Sounds like you have enough Christmas spirit for both of us,' she said dryly but smiled begrudgingly so he sensed the smallest of thaws.

Théo grinned. She had a great sense of humour. 'Since I changed the venue to Château Bijou,' he explained, eager to keep her talking, 'it's kind of become a whole-day event.'

'Sounds very…debauched,' she said with mocking raised eyebrows. But there was a flicker of excitement and curiosity in her stare and she wasn't walking away.

'Not really,' he said, with a smile. 'I was approached by a local special needs school looking for a venue to host their Christmas grotto. I was happy to help, giving them access to the old converted stables. There are stalls and games and a sensory experience and, of course, Père Noël pays a visit. Last year, I even donned the red suit and beard myself when our Santa double-booked himself.'

Connie's eyes widened with surprise as if he'd given her a debauched version of events.

'Then in the evening I host the traditional Christmas *réveillon*,' he went on, addicted to how they could challenge each other and the resultant sparks. 'Lots of delicious food and good company. Tris usually organises games and dancing. I think he'd love to have you there this year, if you can bring yourself to attend. And it goes without saying that there's enough guest rooms at the *château* for you to stay the night if you want.'

His heart thumped at the idea of having her in his home. A chance for a fresh start. He brushed his excitement aside, telling himself he was simply laying the foundations for future years when Connie might bring the baby.

'So you're basically running Christmas HQ now?' she said teasingly, her eyes bright with mirth. 'Sprinkling magic and good cheer wherever you go.'

'Not really.' His heart thudded that he'd managed to draw out her playful side. 'But I do enjoy seeing everyone have a good time. And this year will be special as Théo and Victor will have tied the knot by then. Their first Christmas as a married couple.'

Deciding he'd pleaded his case as well as he could, he held up his hands and stepped back. 'Just think about it. I'll email through the invitation. It should be a magical night and who knows?

By then, you might have some baby news to celebrate.'

He glanced down to her stomach. When he looked back up she was staring again, her eyes shining and her lips parted. His attention lingered on their glossy curves, the fullness and softness he could almost taste. A moment of silent understanding seemed to pass between them, that nagging pull of attraction as if they were each aware that before things had gone wrong, they'd sparked off each other like a lit box of fireworks.

'Well, goodnight, Connie. See you tomorrow.' He forced himself to move away, clinging to the relief that they might find a way to finally put their misunderstandings and animosity behind them and one day be friends.

As he headed down the corridor towards the exit, telling himself to proceed with caution because there was more at stake now than simple sexual tension, she called after him.

'Night, Théo.'

Théo waved over his shoulder but kept his eyes front and centre, the slight hesitation he'd heard in her voice and the feel of her eyes on him making him wonder if they'd ever be able to set aside their chemistry.

CHAPTER FIVE

Three weeks to Christmas

FOR THE PAST week Connie had hardly seen Théo at the hospital beyond catching sight of him on the surgical ward or in the theatre staffroom grabbing a coffee between operations. Rather than feel comforted from having time to put all of their conversations into perspective, she'd reluctantly needed to reassess most of her impressions of the man, an inconvenient state of affairs that left her mildly Théo-obsessed.

His honesty about their attraction, his protectiveness for Tris, his openness about his heartbreaking childhood. Tris never talked to Connie about their father. The one time Connie had asked, he'd said he had no interest in looking for a man who'd walked out on his beloved Maman before he was even born. But, of course, Tris had grown up with Théo as protector and male role model, whereas Théo, it seemed, had had no one, a thought that left Connie desperate to learn more about the man she couldn't seem to brush from her mind.

Now, having just finished seeing her final outpatient of the morning, she was heading for her office to grab a quick bite of lunch when her phone rang. Without checking the caller ID, she answered.

'Connie Dubois,' she said, leaving the outpatient department and taking the stairs to the floor above.

'Dr Dubois, this is Marcel Roulet from Fertility First.'

'Hello.' Connie paused midway up the first flight of stairs, her mind calculating the dates. Maybe this was the follow-up call she'd been expecting from the clinic, not that she'd had time to take the pregnancy test yet. She'd planned to do it first thing tomorrow morning.

'I'm um…calling with an apology,' Roulet said, his voice high pitched with worrying tension. 'I'm afraid there was an incident last week at the clinic on the day you attended for your procedure.'

'Okay…' Connie glanced at her watch, aware she had only a ten-minute window to grab some lunch before she needed to meet her registrar, Jules, for a ward round.

'Yes, there was a clerical error, I'm afraid.'

'I'm sorry, Mr Roulet,' Connie said, retaking the stairs, 'I'm at work at the moment. Could you perhaps pop your reason for calling into an email and I'll look at it when I can?'

'Oh, no, I can't do that,' the man said, the urgency in his voice rising. 'You see, I'm actually calling to inform you that, due to a mistake at our end, I'm afraid you were given the wrong deposit during your insemination procedure.'

Connie froze and gripped the stair rail, lightheaded with shock. 'What?' Had she heard him correctly? Had he really just dropped that bombshell as casually as saying *we gave you the wrong appointment time*?

'I know, it's most irregular,' Roulet added in total understatement. 'I can only apologise profusely and reassure you that we are looking into how this mistake happened.' She heard him swallow. 'I wondered if you'd had chance to confirm a pregnancy or not yet?'

Connie snorted in angry disbelief. She could almost hear his mind working. If she wasn't pregnant, their *mistake* wouldn't matter. They'd be in the clear.

'No,' she said, tightly. 'I was planning on taking a test tomorrow. After day ten, you said.' She dragged in a calming breath, her mind racing as she tried to make sense of his call. 'So I didn't get my friend's sperm. Is that what you're telling me?'

Her heart banged from adrenaline. How could this have happened? What would she tell Tris? Although from a selfish perspective, while regrettable, for Connie it wouldn't be the end of the world. Before Tris had volunteered to be her donor, she'd considered using one of the clinic's anonymous donors instead.

'No, I'm afraid not,' Roulet confirmed flatly.

'So whose sperm did I receive?' she snapped, before chewing at her lip as she considered all the implications. Tris was unlikely to be devastated given he didn't want a family of his own. But it was still an embarrassing and inconvenient situation. Having Tris's baby had felt safe. They were best friends. There was less risk of misaligned expectations. She'd even imagined that one day, when the child was old enough to understand, she would tell her little one that dear Uncle Tris was its father.

'I'm afraid,' Roulet said, 'that due to Fertility First's privacy policy, I can't disclose that information until I've spoken to the donor.'

Connie wanted to laugh. But there was nothing funny about this situation.

'So now you're dotting the i's and crossing the t's,' she said drolly. 'Why didn't you speak to him first, before calling me with such…inconvenient news?'

She understood that mistakes happened, although she'd never imagined they'd happen at a fertility clinic of all places, but she was losing her patience with this man.

'I haven't been able to get hold of the donor

concerned yet,' he said, 'but as soon as I have his consent to disclose his identity, I'll be back in touch.'

'Great,' Connie said dryly. 'Presumably if the procedure wasn't successful and I'm not pregnant, you're off the hook.'

There was a squeak of nervous laughter. 'I really am terribly sorry, Dr Dubois. Needless to say, we have launched a full review of all our procedures and safeguards so we can identify how this error was made and avoid a recurrence in the future. I'll call you back soon, unless you have any other questions for me at this stage.'

'None that would be helpful,' Connie said tightly, her jaw clenched.

'In that case, good day.'

After washing up following a long morning of routine surgeries, Théo collected his phone from Reception and left Theatres. Six missed calls from an external number. Strange. Someone really wanted to get hold of him.

On his way upstairs to his office, he dialled the number to return the call. Théo had taken the two flights of stairs when the call connected and a man answered.

'This is Théo Augustin returning your calls.' Théo pushed through the doors at the top of the stairs, turned left towards his office.

'Mr Augustin,' the man said, his voice carrying a sense of urgency and relief. 'I'm so glad to finally get hold of you.'

'It's Dr Augustin,' Théo said. 'What can I do for you?'

'My name is Marcel Roulet, Clinical Director of the Fertility First clinic.'

Théo smiled. 'I'm a spinal surgeon, Mr Roulet. I think you might have the wrong number.' Wait...fertility clinic. Maybe the guy was after Tris.

'No, I definitely need to speak to you,' Roulet said, sounding increasingly flustered.

'Are you sure you don't want Dr Tristan Augustin? He's a doctor here at St Raphaël Hospital, too.'

There was a beat of silence that made the hairs stand on the back of Théo's neck with foreboding.

'You donated a sample some years ago,' Roulet said hesitantly.

That caught Théo's attention. He froze outside his office, unease coiling in his stomach. 'I did. Many years ago, but I assumed you'd thrown it out. You never contacted me to confirm it had been used.'

Was this guy calling to tell him his sperm had finally been defrosted, after all this time?

'I'm afraid I need to inform you of a procedural error here at the clinic, sir. You see, we had two donors with very similar names...'

Théo's head began to buzz with the sound of

white noise. He braced his hand on the door jamb and locked his knees, trying to remain upright while half listening to the man drone on about his regrets and apologies and reassurances that *this kind of mix-up would never happen again.*

Théo closed his eyes, the implications of this call hitting him like a shock wave following an explosion. He knew what was coming next. What were the chances that his sperm had been mixed up with another man's the week that Tris, whose name was similar to Théo's, had donated so that independent, go-it-alone Connie could have a child?

Just then, with Roulet still nervously prattling in his ear, clearly building up to the big reveal, Théo became aware of movement nearby. He glanced up. Connie left the ladies' room and crossed the corridor, heading for her office a few doors down from his.

She spied him. Their eyes met. A polite but hesitant smile tugged at her lovely lips. That surge of connection that always came struck him in the solar plexus and he almost laughed at its utter irrelevance. How ironic that as they finally seemed to have brokered a truce and agreed to put their sexual chemistry behind them and get along for Tris's sake, fate had thrown them a monumental cock-up.

Seeing him frozen in place with the phone to

his ear, Connie ducked into her office and quietly closed the door.

Dread settled in the pit of Théo's stomach as he tuned back into Roulet's apologies and excuses.

'Enough,' he said, reeling. He had questions for the man. Lots of questions. And a bad feeling that he wouldn't like any of the answers. And nor would Connie.

CHAPTER SIX

HAVING RETURNED FROM the bathroom to her office, Connie stared down at the test on her desk, her eyes stinging with happy tears. It was positive. It had worked. She was going to have a baby.

Covering her mouth with her hand, she smothered a delighted giggle. After everything she'd been through in her personal life with Guy and then Théo, finally something was going her way. Automatically, she picked up her phone to text Tris the news, but then remembered the baby wasn't his and hesitated, her joy diminished.

Would her friend be upset that he wasn't the father after all? She hoped not, given he'd decided against raising children of his own, but she chewed at her lip worriedly all the same. Tris's friendship had seen Connie through some tough times in the past. They were always there for each other, through heartache and work dilemmas and for the good times. All she could do was tell him about the mix-up and hope he would continue to support her the way he always had.

Before she could call him to explain the bizarre turn of events and the news she'd received from the clinic, there was a knock at the door. Connie stood and pulled it open, surprised to see Théo standing there wearing a dark and worrying frown.

'What's wrong?' she asked, her heart thudding at both his proximity and his ashen complexion. He'd obviously been in the middle of a serious-looking phone call just now. 'Is it a patient?'

He shook his head and stepped into her office. 'I need to talk to you.'

Slightly miffed by his abruptness, Connie closed the door. Her office seemed too small with him in it. His big sexy body encroaching on her personal space and making her all too aware she was a woman who hadn't had sex for almost three years. She brushed that thought aside and turned to face him. He was staring at the pregnancy test on the desk.

Connie flushed, embarrassed, and stepped in front of her desk, blocking the test from his sight. She should have thought to hide it before answering the door. But Théo already knew she might be having Tristan's baby.

'Is it positive?' he asked darkly, his glittering stare locked to hers and his body emanating a kind of coiled energy as if he was still looking out for his brother's welfare and convinced Connie would somehow hurt Tris. And maybe now, through no fault of her own, she might.

Defensive, Connie raised her chin. 'Yes. Not that it's really any of your business. So you can put away the scowl.' Because of the mistake at the clinic, the baby was wholly Connie's. He wouldn't be Uncle Théo. He wouldn't need to worry about Tris's parental rights.

'I disagree,' he said, inching closer so her heart leapt excitedly and her body temperature spiked.

Still, Connie rolled her eyes in exasperation. 'Don't start all that Uncle Théo stuff again…'

While the possessive glint in his eyes thrilled the part of her still desperately attracted to him, she knew she should tell him that he wouldn't in fact be related to her child. But she owed it to her friend to speak to Tris first. She didn't want him finding out from anyone else but her.

'Tell me,' Théo said, shoving his hands into his trouser pockets as he pinned her with his intense, impassioned stare, 'does the name Marcel Roulet mean anything to you?'

While his voice was calm, steely determination shone in his eyes as he inched closer, watching her mouth, waiting for her answer.

More heat flamed in Connie's cheeks at his line of questioning. Had Tris already been contacted about the mix-up at the clinic? Did Théo already know Connie seemed to have chosen the world's most incompetent fertility clinic for her procedure? Was he here to berate her for messing Tris around? And why, when this had turned into some sort of farce, when she had her ward round to get to, was she still exquisitely aware of Théo's manliness and raw sex appeal?

'I know him,' she admitted carefully, blaming her hormones. 'But I told you last night, this is between me and Tris. When are you going to stop parenting him? He's a grown man. He's about to be married. He has his life far better sorted than either you or I,' she scoffed.

'Tris is my brother,' Théo said, his eyes narrowing. 'The only family I have.'

'I know…' Connie winced, compassion for him coming unbidden and once more sending her off balance.

'I'll never stop looking out for his welfare and happiness,' he went on, in that same eerily calm voice. 'But that's beside the point. Are you expecting a call from this Marcel Roulet by any chance?'

Connie huffed, embracing her anger at his intrusive questions over the irrelevant lust she couldn't seem to escape when he was around. 'Again, none of your business.' But how did Théo know that?

'Unless it *is* my business.' He moved closer, into her personal space, his stare shifting over her face, once more dropping to her mouth where she was slack-jawed in disbelief at his effrontery.

Stunned by the giddy tingle in her lips, as if he'd done more than stare, she glared back. 'And why would it be anything to do with you?' She fisted her hands on her hips, her annoyance finally piqued even as her pulse flew at his closeness and the wild, protective look in his eyes. It made her shudder deliciously, the way she had when she'd climaxed crushed in his strong arms that night. She had the highly inappropriate and thrilling thought that he might touch her or kiss her again. But she couldn't possibly actually want that, could she? She was having a baby. Another man's baby. This…*thing* with Théo, whatever it was, should be the last thing on her mind.

Théo smiled but there was no warmth in the expression. Only determination and that heated kind of hunger she wasn't sure was real or a figment of her hormonal imagination.

'Because I too spoke to Mr Roulet this morning,' he said, glancing down at her stomach.

Ridiculously, Connie placed her hand there to shield the baby from his possessive gaze.

'And from what he said,' Théo went on, his cool tone in stark contrast to the flames in his eyes, 'I'm almost one hundred per cent certain that your baby is also mine.'

Connie gaped, too stunned to laugh in his face at the absurdity of his outlandish claim. 'Don't be ridiculous,' she muttered finally, Marcel Roulet's words trickling through her panicked mind.

...a clerical error...the wrong deposit...can't disclose that information until I've spoken to the donor.

'No…no,' Connie whispered, slumping into a chair before she lost all strength in her legs. 'You're crazy. Why would it be your baby?' It didn't make sense.

She looked to Théo in desperation, willing him to laugh and say it was all a prank, willing him to say there was no way it could be his child because he'd never visited a fertility clinic. But instead his face hardened.

'Because I sold my sperm, years ago when I was an impoverished medical student,' he confirmed. 'They mixed up the samples. Clearly having two *T Augustins* on the books was too much for the clinic's primitive filing system.' He snorted and shook his head in disgust.

Was it true? Why would he lie? He would never play a trick this cruel on Tris.

'This isn't funny,' Connie said automatically, clinging to the hope that she'd received another donor's sperm and not Théo's. The last thing she wanted was to have *his* baby, especially given their past animosity and current pretty rampant sexual tension. She could just about tolerate working with him. How on earth would she survive raising a child with him and not go mad?

Because where Tris had been happy to take a back seat in the baby's life and watch from afar, she had a bad feeling that perfect-family-obsessed Théo would want to be intimately involved in his child's upbringing. Which meant also being involved in Connie's life.

'At last we agree,' he said, his tone sarcastic but his expression serious. 'It's not funny at all, Connie.'

'Maybe…it wasn't your sperm,' she reasoned hopefully, clinging to any hope she could muster. She didn't want to do this with him. She'd planned to do it alone.

Théo shot her a pitying look. 'We'll soon see. But if this baby is mine, that changes everything.' He leaned closer so she saw predatory sparks in his impassioned eyes. 'You can forget your plan to raise my child alone.'

'*Our* child,' Connie pointed out automatically. Her breathing sped up excitedly as she watched him inch closer, his stare bouncing between hers and her mouth so her lips tingled harder and her breath gusted and she felt certain he was about to kiss her.

'I'm not my brother,' he continued, resting his hands on the arms of her chair, looming over her so she had to crane her neck to keep eye contact, 'happy for you to raise our baby by yourself. I'm going to want more. To be a real father to our child as it deserves. To be there for every birthday, every Christmas, every school play and parents' evening. You're going to see a whole lot more of me than you want and you'll just have to get used to that.'

Connie opened her mouth to deny him but she was too shocked to speak. Ludicrously, with total disregard for timing or relevance, her body was achingly turned on. By him!

'No. This can't be happening,' she muttered when he moved away. 'It must be a mistake. It wasn't supposed to be this way. It wasn't supposed to involve you.' He must be deluded or misinformed.

Théo cast her a withering, slightly pitying look as if he'd somehow slotted all the pieces of this mix-up together long before Connie.

Then, with impeccable timing that made Connie feel as insignificant as a pawn on a giant cosmic chessboard being manoeuvred by malicious higher forces, her phone rang and her stomach dropped like a stone.

Connie hung up the call, which had obviously been from the fertility clinic, the pallor of her skin confirming Théo's worst suspicions. Earlier, he'd given Marcel Roulet permission to inform the recipient of his identity. One look at Connie's devastation told him that she finally believed what Théo had already guessed.

The clinic had switched Tris's specimen for his. Connie was carrying Théo's baby.

'I can't believe this,' she whispered, staring at

him accusingly as if he'd deliberately tricked her or telepathically impregnated her or somehow engineered the specimen switch.

'My entire reason for doing it this way,' she went on angrily, 'was because I'm not interested in dealing with all that relationship stuff but I wanted a child. But now there's you to deal with.' She shot him an accusing look, as if he and the man who'd hurt and betrayed her were one and the same.

'Maybe it's a lesson for us both,' he muttered darkly, aware she was simply lashing out. 'We have the consequences without having experienced the joy of the conception. Maybe babies should be made the old-fashioned way...'

But a part of him experienced the first trembles of excitement that he was actually, finally going to be a father. After all the heartache with Anaïs, who'd changed her mind about having a child with him, after his own abandonment and tumultuous childhood, here was a chance for a fresh start. Only hot on the heels of that thought, protective urges surged inside him like tidal waves. For Tris, whose role in all this had now been discarded. For the baby, who, like Théo and Tris, would grow up in a fractured family. Even for Connie herself, who looked pale with shock.

Once she'd processed his offhand comment, her wounded gaze flew to his. 'The old-fashioned way didn't work out for me. Despite the plans and promises we made, my ex-fiancé preferred to impregnate one of his office colleagues while I pursued my surgical career. This way, I could have a family to my own timeline and without having to trust someone unworthy. Without getting my heart broken in the process. But it wasn't supposed to involve anyone else, least of all you.'

Théo winced as fear replaced the compassion he felt for Connie. When he'd sold his specimen all those years ago, he'd signed a waiver renouncing his legal responsibilities for any child conceived. But if Connie decided to exclude him, he would fight to be a part of their child's life, knowing as he did what it was like to grow up without a father.

As they locked stares, each processing the news and battling their own doubts, that damned connection of theirs crackled, drawing them together as if they were puppets and fate were laughing while pulling their strings.

'And yet here we are,' he said, desperately clinging to his composure. 'Ironic considering you wanted nothing to do with me.' Of course, he could understand she'd been hurt and deceived in the past, but Théo wasn't that man.

Dragging in a deep breath, he tried to apply logic to the situation. 'But whatever you planned, however much you wished to ignore me, all that is irrelevant now.'

'What does that mean?' she asked, clearly still stunned by the news and emotionally guarded.

'It means,' he said, his heart pounding with fear that she had all the power here, 'that family is everything to me, as I told you. I'm not going to lose out on a relationship with my child just because you can't forgive me and planned to do this alone. A child needs to know its father, so don't go thinking you can dismiss me or sweep my feelings aside or conveniently cut me out of the picture.'

She gripped the arms of the chair and leaned forward. 'Do *you* even want a baby?' she asked with a frown. 'You're almost forty and single. Are you sure you want to go down this track?'

Théo gaped in disbelief. 'I assume by *down this track* you mean being a parent to my own child. I've always wanted a family of my own. One of the reasons my marriage ended was because Anaïs changed her mind. I never imagined it would happen this way or with you, but I fully intend to father our child. You might take your big boisterous family for granted, but you know my past, know that I never knew my own father. All children should know they are loved and accepted by both parents.'

'You're right. I'm sorry…' She deflated and looked away, blinking rapidly as if she might cry. 'I would never stop you having a relationship with the baby, just like I'd never have stopped Tris.'

Her voice broke and compassion swamped him. He stepped closer, took another deep breath and softened his tone. 'Look, I might have…overreacted just now…marching in here. This has been a terrible shock for us both. But I should have got a hold of my composure first or let you discover the news from Roulet.'

He could admit he was highly sensitive to any perceived threat to those he loved. The minute he'd put all of the pieces together, his first thought, after concern that Tris might be upset that he wasn't the father after all, was that Connie hated him and he was about to lose his child even before it was born.

She sniffed and nodded but wouldn't look at him.

Théo sought the calm he used in the operating room. 'If we're mature and respectful of each other,' he went on, trying to hide the desperation from his voice, 'we can figure this out together. At least the procedure worked and you got what you wanted: a baby.'

'Yes…' She kept her gaze down, still appearing dazed and numb.

Théo poured her a glass of water and set it on the desk. 'Drink this for the shock. Doctor's orders.'

When she smiled thinly and meekly obeyed he went on, soothingly. 'I know you think it's easier to do this alone after the hurt and betrayal you've been through, but I'm not that man, Connie.' He wasn't asking for her trust, just a chance to be involved. 'Surely when it comes to parenting, two heads are better than one.'

She sipped, silently nodding, albeit reluctantly.

Because his legs felt weak, he pulled up a seat opposite hers. 'How are you feeling, physically?' he asked, cautiously, trying to put himself in her shoes. He'd not only hurt her in the past, he'd also stormed back into her life and discovered that the baby she'd thought she'd be raising alone was his, not Tris's.

'Fine.' She sipped the water, her hand trembling, peering at him with lingering doubt. 'Absolutely fine.'

'Now that the question of the paternity is resolved,' he said, trying on a half-smile to make light of the crazy situation none of them could have foreseen, 'I think congratulations are in order.' He jerked his chin towards the pregnancy test on the desk and reached for her hand, ignoring the thud of his heart at the contact and how a part of him wanted to hold her, to reassure her everything would work out, to make her see that he wouldn't let her or their child down. Ever.

'Thanks,' she muttered, swallowing hard, the tiniest of smiles tugging at her lips. 'You too, I guess.'

'Look, just because neither of us planned this,' he said quietly, staring into her deep brown intelligent eyes, 'doesn't mean we can't make it work for everyone.' Connie was a caring compassionate woman. If he looked past his own fear, he felt confident she would do the right thing and put the baby's needs first. 'The most important person to consider is the one you're now carrying. That's all that matters, don't you agree?'

'I do.' She nodded, seeming to pull herself together as she looked up.

For a few seconds, while his pulse buzzed in his ears, Théo sat trapped in the moment. Her hand was warm and soft in his. Her big eyes swam with emotion behind their long lashes. Her mouth, only inches away from his, parted as her breaths gusted in rapid little pants he just couldn't ignore.

'I need to get back to work,' she whispered, not pulling her hand away.

Théo nodded. 'Me too.'

What was he thinking? Just because he had all these protective urges, didn't mean he could indulge his attraction to Connie. It was still irrelevant, maybe even more so now that she was having his baby. She didn't trust him and he would do anything to safeguard his relationship with his child, and, by extension, Connie.

Reluctantly, he let go of her hand and pushed back his chair to give her some space. He stood, planning to leave her to mull things over in private while he did the same, but her phone rang again.

She snatched it up and answered, slipping on her work persona before his eyes. 'Okay. Yes.' She glanced his way meaningfully, a small frown tugging at her lips. 'I'll be right there.'

When she'd hung up, she stood and reached for her stethoscope. 'Elodie Verdier's condition is deteriorating. My registrar thinks she might have sepsis.'

'Then let's go see her together,' he said, grateful to have something to think about beyond the fact that, astonishingly, he and Connie were having a baby together when they'd only had sex that one time three years ago.

They rushed to the post-op ward where they met Connie's registrar, Jules.

'Elodie Verdier spiked a fever during the night and was commenced on antibiotics,' Jules said, speaking rapidly. 'I organised a repeat X-ray and scan this morning, but she's been deteriorating throughout the day. Her blood pressure is low, the fever is high, her urine output is reduced and she's showing signs of delirium.'

Théo and Connie hurried to the patient's bedside while the registrar continued to relay blood-test results. Since they'd reviewed the patient the day before, she'd clearly deteriorated rapidly. Now her skin was grey, her breathing rapid behind an oxygen mask and she seemed confused, unaware of who they were or where she was.

'Roll her, please,' Connie asked the nursing

staff, who rolled Elodie onto her side so she could listen to her lungs.

Théo took her pulse and auscultated her heart from the front, then checking the wounds for signs of infection.

'Have you taken blood for culture?' he asked Jules. If they knew what pathogen they were dealing with, they'd have a better chance of treating the infection.

The registrar nodded. 'The doctor who started the antibiotics took them overnight, and I've repeated them this morning. No results back yet.'

When Connie finished her examination, they left the room to discuss their findings.

'The heart sounds are normal,' Théo said, looking to Connie.

'And the chest is clear,' Connie added, frowning with concern. 'But she's clearly in septic shock. We should transfer her to Intensive Care.'

Jules nodded, making notes.

'The scan should show us if there's a collection or haematoma internally,' Théo said, impressed that he and Connie could set aside their shocking revelations of the morning and collaborate so effectively.

'Again, I'm waiting for those results,' Jules said.

'We could head down to Radiology,' Connie suggested, looking to Théo for his nod of agreement. 'Speak to the radiologist and try to expedite the results.'

'Yes. Let's do that.' He addressed Jules once more. 'You speak to ICU. Insert a central line and start some vasopressin for her hypotension. We need to get her stabilised in case we need to take her back to Theatre.'

Then, without further mention of the momentous events that had transpired in their personal lives, he and Connie hurried to the radiology department, once more a team of sorts.

CHAPTER SEVEN

LATER THAT EVENING, having checked up on Elodie on ICU and found her patient in a stable condition, Connie left the surgical floor and headed for the hospital's rear staff exit. After an unbelievable and emotional day, she was mentally and physically exhausted and looking forward to sleep to reset her brain. In true denial, she couldn't even contemplate thinking about Théo and the implications of the baby being his until she'd eaten dinner, taken a long soak in the bath and had a full night's sleep.

Maybe tomorrow, everything would once more make sense… With any luck, she'd wake up to find it had all been a bad dream.

The lift doors opened on the ground floor. On autopilot, Connie stepped out and found herself greeted with the enchanting sound of a choir singing at the entrance to the children's ward. A crowd of patients, staff and visitors had gathered to listen to the beautiful harmonised singing.

Smiling, Connie joined the crowd, taking comfort from the well-known children's songs about wintertime, Christmas trees and Papa Noël. Her troubled mind eased as the familiar melodies reminded her that Christmas was right around the corner. This time next year, she'd have a baby and all the excitement and wonder of its first Christmas to celebrate. But it was also Théo's baby. He would want to be involved and she couldn't for one second deny him, regardless of their messy past and her reasons for choosing to do this alone, just as she wouldn't have denied Tris a relationship with his son or daughter. He'd been through enough heartache and uncertainty with his childhood and his divorce. When he'd talked about a child needing its father, Connie's heart had almost split in two. She'd never really considered the full impact of Tris and Théo's upbringing from Théo's perspective.

And Théo wasn't her ex. He was a decent man who cared deeply about people: his patients and Tris especially. And after everything he'd lost—his father, his mother and grandmother and his marriage and hopes of children—he deserved family. He was certainly right about a child deserving to know they were safe and loved and cherished by both parents.

Overwhelmed once more, Connie sighed. Everything was such a mess. Earlier, within the space of minutes, she'd gone from delight that she was having the baby she'd wanted, to having to share it with Théo of all people. But surely if she and Théo could trust each other in the operating room and when it came to the patients in their care, they could come to some sort of suitable co-parenting arrangement that would satisfy them both.

As if he'd heard her thoughts, Théo materialised at her side. Dressed in St Raphaël navy-blue scrubs, he too appeared a little fatigued, his dark hair a little ruffled, presumably from wearing a surgical hat.

'Hi,' she whispered, getting lost in his eyes and the intense way he looked at her, as if to him she were a fascinating stranger who happened to be carrying his baby. And in many ways they were strangers. They might have intimate knowledge of each other's bodies, but, up to now, she'd deliberately avoided getting to know him better. Suddenly, the shocking events of the day meant she had questions. Lots of questions. About his foster parents, his marriage breakdown and his world view, which was likely different from Tris's given Théo was older and had always tried to protect Tris. But who had been looking out for Théo?

'Hi.' He smiled, his stare clouded by uncertainty as if he too had more he wanted to say. Then, taking her by surprise, Théo joined in with the choir and the crowd, singing along to the well-known songs in a deep baritone while flicking her the kind of playful smile that made her breath catch.

Connie chuckled to herself when he sang with even greater enthusiasm, grinning her way unselfconsciously. But that was Théo. A man comfortable enough in his own skin that there was no pretence. He could admit his mistakes and apologise. He fought fiercely and passionately for those he loved. All admirable qualities.

As the festive music swirled around them, things seemed surmountable once more. Connie surrendered and sang along too, grateful for the few moments of joyous distraction from what had been an overwhelming day.

When the song came to an end, she and Théo stepped aside. 'I've been in Theatre all afternoon and I'm on call tonight,' he said quietly as, together, they walked towards the exit. 'Have you managed to review our ICU patient?'

Connie nodded, aware that his concern for Elodie matched her own. Connie brought him up to speed on Elodie's progress as they left the hospital and paused outside. 'Her blood pressure has stabilised. Test results show it's an atypical bacterial infection.' The scans had shown a small paraspinal collection of fluid, which for now didn't seem to be compressing any nerves and might resolve on its own. 'I suggest we watch and wait.'

She moved just beyond the exit, away from the busy comings and goings through the electronic doors. Connie glanced down at her feet, her emotions all over the place once more. As Elodie's lead surgeon, she couldn't help but feel responsible for the post-op infection.

'Don't blame yourself,' Théo said, somehow sensing her feelings. 'Infection is always a risk with any surgery. We were both responsible for Elodie, and we did everything right.'

Connie nodded, grateful for his words of comfort. 'I know.'

'I'll look in on her later,' Théo said, his breath forming a cloud in the frigid winter air. 'Look, I know we have other things to discuss, but you should go home,' he added, his stare softening with compassion. 'Get some sleep. You look tired and it's been an emotional roller coaster of a day that neither of us were expecting.'

Choked by his understanding and ashamed by her earlier overreaction and by all the things she'd said to him since he'd started working at St Raphaël, Connie nodded. 'You're right. It has.' A patient unwell enough to need ICU, the fertility clinic mix-up, discovering Théo not Tris was the father of her baby...

'I'm sorry...for earlier,' she said, forcing herself to meet his warm stare. 'For the way I acted. I was knocked sideways with shock. I said things...'

As she looked up at him, a flood of questions rushed her mind. How on earth would they make this work? What were his expectations when it came to the baby? And perhaps most pressing— how could she switch off this insistent thrill of attraction, when she had way bigger issues on which to focus?

As if he could read her mind, Théo's expression softened further. 'It's all going to be okay, Connie. I promise.' He stepped closer and rested his hand on her shoulder so familiar heat spread through her veins. 'We'll figure it out together.'

'I hope so.' Connie glanced at her feet and nodded, even though she didn't fully share his confidence. The last time she'd trusted a man's promise, it had been one of Guy's and it had broken as easily as a bird's egg. But Théo's touch was comforting and she didn't need to trust him with her emotions. Just her baby. *Their* baby.

'Thanks,' she said, blinking up at him as her heart fluttered. 'For saying the right things today and for your apology last week. It means a lot. I should have confronted you about what I'd overheard that morning sooner. Cleared the air. I just…' She looked down again, ashamed. 'Well, my trust had been badly damaged and I was a mess too. But you were right. I did overreact, back then and on your first day. I'm sorry.'

'It's okay,' he said, his hand gently squeezing her shoulder. 'I understand what you've been through. Look, if you're free tomorrow, we could talk then, away from here.' He dropped his hand and Connie reeled, instantly missing his touch.

'About the baby and how we're going to do this. It might be wise to speak before we get caught up in Tris and Victor's wedding the weekend after.'

'Okay. That sounds sensible,' she said, aware that it was cold and, unlike her, he wasn't wearing a coat. 'I need to figure out how I'm going to tell Tris that the baby isn't his.'

But maybe because they'd had such an emotional day, maybe because she was having his baby, maybe because she was in no rush to be alone with her tumultuous thoughts and she'd seen a more human side to him this evening—a man singing rousing Christmas songs for sick kids—she couldn't make her feet move.

She didn't need to rely on anyone. But if she had to, a man like Théo—responsible, moral and selfless—would be her man of choice.

'We can figure out how to tell Tris tomorrow too if you like. Do you want me to call you a ride?' he said, unmoving.

Connie shook her head, her confusion building. 'I'm happy on the *Métro*.' So why was she lingering, her body still abuzz from his touch? Why were those stubborn memories of how electrifying their first kiss had been spinning in her head? Why was her body inching towards his as if she was about to do something reckless?

'Goodnight, then,' he said finally, his hand returning to her shoulder as he swooped in to press his lips first to one cheek, then the other in the French way.

The gesture was almost automatic, but as he lingered in her personal space as if he couldn't bear to step back, Connie's breathing stalled. The warmth and scent of him that close made her heart race with longing. Before she knew what she was doing, she turned her face to his and their lips grazed in the barest of tentative kisses.

Thrilling excitement slammed through her. For a loaded-with-possibility second, Théo stilled apart from his fingers, which curled around her shoulder possessively. His heated stare, locked to hers, darkened and made Connie feel naked. That connection she'd been fighting since he'd walked back into her life, there between them since the first time they met, built stronger than ever and harder to deny because now they would always be connected through the life growing inside Connie.

Tired of fighting her attraction to him and because she knew from past experience how good it would feel, Connie surged up on her tiptoes as Théo swooped in to capture her lips with his. Desperate to switch off her mind's incessant questioning, Connie pressed her cold lips to his warm ones, losing herself in the kick of safe physical desire.

It felt so good to surrender, to feel desired by someone she knew wasn't looking for a relationship. Someone who knew her history, understood her priorities were the pregnancy and the baby. Someone with whom she was safe to just be a woman attracted to a man without agenda.

Adrenaline surged through her system, shunting her heart rate higher as Théo held her close. His kiss turned quickly bold and commanding, his lips moving against hers as if he'd been dreaming of doing this for days. As if he too were powerless.

Dangerously, Connie slid her hands around the back of his neck, her fingertips grazing his hairline, and parted her lips against his, a tiny moan escaping her throat as the kiss deepened in an erotic tangle of lips and tongues and panted breath. Théo's arms hauled her closer so her body was pressed to his hard chest, hard thighs, the start of an erection grazing her hip.

A moment's doubt rushed her mind. She shouldn't be doing this. Kissing him in the hospital car park, making herself more turned on than she'd felt in three years. It wasn't fair to send him mixed messages. But she had mixed emotions. It was as Théo had said earlier—they had the consequences of a baby without having experienced the thrill of making it. And it would have been thrilling. Sexually, she and Théo just clicked.

In that second, with their lips still locked and their hearts racing side by side, the nearby hospital doors slid open and the sound of the choir singing *'Vive le Vent'*, the French version of 'Jingle Bells' grew louder, the upbeat catchy tune drifting out to break the spell. Snapped from the madness of practically making out with Théo in the hospital car park, Connie pulled back, her heart racing erratically and her regrets warming her cheeks.

Théo looked as dazed as she felt, his fierce expression in stark contrast to the jolly Christmas song, which told the story of the winter wind and an old man walking in the snow. Their eyes met as they each caught their frosty breaths. The absurdity of the moment struck Connie and she laughed, giggling harder when Théo joined in, pressing his lips swiftly to her forehead and then sliding his hands from her waist and stepping back.

With the tension snapped and the moment broken, Connie ran a hand through her hair, trying to pull herself together. 'I think you're right. I should go home and get some sleep. I'm acting emotionally. That probably wasn't a good idea.'

Although for some reason, maybe because they'd slept together before and neither of them was denying their attraction no matter how badly it complicated things, she couldn't bring herself to apologise for the kiss. She didn't regret it. It had happened in the moment. Call it Christmas madness. A response to fatigue and worry and the romance of the silly season, just like the last time she'd behaved recklessly and slept with him.

'I'll see you tomorrow,' he said, a ghost of that gorgeous smile on his lips and unmistakeable hunger and disappointment in his eyes.

Connie turned away before she could once more succumb to temptation, casually waving over her shoulder. But as she crossed the car park, her senses were on high alert as if he was watching her retreat. At the last minute, before she left the hospital grounds, she glanced back.

He was where she'd left him, still observing with an inscrutable expression. Still handsome and vulnerable and looking as confused as Connie felt. Still making her blood hot as if she had her own portable central heating system under her coat.

CHAPTER EIGHT

THE NEXT DAY was Saturday. Despite being on call, and after the shocking revelations and that incendiary kiss in the car park, Théo had somehow managed to get a few hours' sleep. Eager to capitalise on their tentative truce and discuss how they would work as parents, he'd arranged to meet Connie, at Rue de Rivoli. She was wrapped up against the cold, her green scarf making her eyes seem brighter and her cautious smile resurfacing all those protective urges of his, and he had pressed a restrained kiss to her cheek and forced himself to behave.

Wanting her physically had become way more complicated. Now there was too much at stake for him to focus solely on their attraction, no matter how rampant. And he couldn't afford to mess this up.

As they walked the city, chatting about inconsequential things and admiring how every street seemed to sparkle with twinkling lights, every historic square boasted a towering Christmas tree and every shop window glittered with magical Christmas displays, they'd each cautiously acknowledged that they were still reeling from the turn of events and their respective calls from the clinic.

Hoping to explore trickier subjects than Tris's wedding the following weekend and the upcoming Christmas festivities, Théo took Connie to one of his favourite cafés for hot chocolate and pastries. Café Solène was located down a cobbled street, well away from the main tourist areas, so they easily found a table in the window and ordered *chocolat chaud* and croissant.

'So,' he said when the waitress departed, resisting the temptation to touch her hand across the table, 'should we talk about that unexpected and incredibly hot kiss last night?' He softened his bold question with a playful smile.

He wasn't naive. He knew it meant nothing. They'd had a highly emotional and shocking day yesterday. But that reckless moment served as an acknowledgement that, regardless of what else was going on between them, if you scratched beneath the surface, their fierce sexual attraction was undeniable.

'I'd rather talk about the baby,' she said, shooting him a good-natured smile. Then her expression became serious.

'Okay,' Théo conceded, surprised that she'd

chosen to broach the main topic on his mind. 'Do you want to start?'

Connie hesitantly looked up from the small Christmas tree at the centre of their table. 'First, I'm curious,' she said, watching him with obvious interest. 'What made you donate all those years ago, when you've clearly always wanted a family of your own?'

Théo dragged in a breath. He rarely looked back, preferring to focus on creating a stable and hopeful future. But for Connie, he would make an exception.

'It was Tris, actually,' Théo said with a shrug, continuing when she frowned in confusion. 'He was about to turn eighteen. Money was tight as we were both in full-time education, him still at school and me at medical school. But he was desperate for the same gaming console all his school friends had.'

As he recalled those difficult years when the weight of responsibility had sometimes felt overwhelming and only highlighted his sense of anger at the father who'd rejected them, his heart thudded. 'And it was worth it. You should have seen his face when he opened my gift. Of course, I never told him how I'd got the money.'

'Wow, Théo…' she said, looking at him with awe as if he'd done something truly special.

'What about you?' Théo asked, changing the subject. 'What made you go down the donor route? Have you really abandoned the search for a committed relationship? You're only thirty-five.'

When she pressed her lips together, her eyes darting away, he quickly added, 'I'm not judging. I understand how devastating it can be when someone you love lets you down. When you had a plan to spend for ever with someone and the other person changed their mind. But you're a smart, attractive woman, Connie. You have an awful lot going for you.' Did she really want to be alone for the rest of her life?

Connie sighed, the stare she levelled on him defiant so he saw the depth of her past hurt and betrayal. 'I told you about my fiancé, Guy,' she said, idly twirling the miniature Christmas tree as if it were part of a wind-up music box. 'What he did—the lies, the double life, taking advantage of my long hours at the hospital—it really damaged my ability to trust.'

'He sounds despicable,' Théo said, furious that anyone would treat caring, gorgeous Connie with such little respect and consideration.

'Yes. But the worst part was that I doubted myself. My instincts. I felt stupid, as if I should have somehow known what was going on if only I'd opened my eyes wider.'

'That's understandable,' he said as soon as the waitress who'd delivered their drinks and croissants departed. 'Everyone would react that way.' He wouldn't patronise her. Connie was an intelligent woman. She would know what her ex had done said nothing about her and everything about his inadequacies.

'With the exception of a drunken rebound one-night stand one Christmas eve,' she added, flicking him a knowing look that heated his blood, 'it took me a long time to date again. Then, when I did pluck up the courage, I just never seemed able to get past a second or third date before seeing all these red flags,' she admitted quietly, stirring her hot chocolate thoughtfully.

'I'm sorry,' he said, fighting the growing urge to touch her. 'My careless comments that morning probably added to your poor impression of men in general.'

She watched him carefully, an insightful gleam in her eyes. 'At least you and I had chemistry,' she said. 'Other men I dated looked great on paper, but when we met in person there was just no spark at all.'

Théo nodded, thinking their sparks could probably ignite the earth's atmosphere.

'Suddenly I was thirty-five and happy to be single,' she went on, when he stayed quiet, absorbing every word as a detective stored away clues. 'I love my job. I have a great apartment, lots of friends, an active social life.'

'But you still wanted a family,' he said, able to empathise. He'd always hoped to have children one day. When Anaïs had left, his dreams of a child of his own had been pushed back, then he'd grown busy with his career and spending time with Tris and Victor and trying to create some semblance of family from the rubble left from his past losses and failed marriage.

Connie nodded, seeming to relax further. 'My friend Chloe, who's a couple of years older than me, had just been diagnosed with lupus and was advised to delay starting a family until it was under control. She'd just got married and had been looking forward to having a baby. I suddenly thought, why am I putting this off? I've reached the top of the career ladder. I'm on my way to forty. None of us knows what is around the corner health-wise… I just felt that it was now or never and I didn't want to find myself in my forties with regrets. Then I talked to Tris about it and he didn't laugh or call me crazy. Instead he offered to be my donor and… Well, you know the rest. Here we are.'

She took a sip of hot chocolate and licked her lips, distracting Théo from his next question with memories of the passion behind their kiss the night before, the urge to kiss her again obliterating all the reasons he shouldn't indulge.

'What about you?' she asked, turning the questions his way. 'What happened with Anaïs?'

'The divorce was by mutual consent,' he began cagily, because opening up wasn't something that came naturally. 'We of course talked about having a family when we first got together. But after we married, Anaïs kept putting it off. We were both busy with work, as you can imagine. You know how demanding surgery can be. On calls, late nights, working the holidays. Anaïs often complained that I was hardly ever there, even when I was home. But she too was chasing promotions and building her real-estate career.'

Connie nodded encouragingly.

'Towards the end, it seemed that every time I raised starting a family, she shut the topic down. It was as if she'd actually decided she didn't want children after all without telling me. Finally, she admitted that she had changed her mind. That she was enjoying her career too much and no longer wanted a family. Not with me. She said I constantly held back from her emotionally.'

'Was she right?' Connie asked, observing him carefully.

'Maybe she had a point.' He shrugged, his barriers rising because he didn't often discuss his feelings, preferring to leave the past behind. 'I didn't see it at the time, but I guess I can be… emotionally cautious, shall we say?'

Maybe he'd overprotected himself from being hurt again after losing his family. But then again, maybe he'd been right to keep those barriers up. His marriage had failed after all, although he'd largely blamed himself.

'Can't we all?' Connie scoffed, flicking him a

sympathetic smile. 'And in your case I can kind of understand why, after what you and Tris went through growing up. Tris doesn't talk about it much, but I suspect you each have a different take on your childhood anyway, from what you've told me. At least Tris had you.'

Théo swallowed, finding Connie easy to talk to but eager to avoid discussing the rejection and losses of his painful past. 'I guess the deal-breaker for Anaïs was my failure to be present in my relationship, for which I take responsibility.'

'And for you it was the issue of children,' she said.

He nodded, relieved he was finally having a child, just not in the traditional way.

'Clearly you and Anaïs wanted different things,' Connie said. 'You can't take all the blame for the relationship ending if she changed her mind about family but kept you dangling.'

'I guess not,' Théo admitted, feeling way too exposed.

'I'm really sorry that it didn't work out for you,' she said, tilting her head in empathy. 'So you haven't been tempted to try to find love again?'

Théo dodged the question. 'I guess we're both quite similar, you and I.' He shrugged, the conversation skating close to his comfort level. 'With the exception of personal relationships, our lives are good. It would take something really special to make us want to take the risk again, don't you agree? And now…well, the baby takes precedence.'

His pulse lurched as she nodded thoughtfully and stared the way she had the night before, just before they'd kissed, as if she saw him more clearly. Théo's temperature soared, that urge to touch her returning.

'What?' he asked finally, licking his top lip, wondering if he had a chocolate moustache.

'Nothing.' She shook her head, but continued to stare enigmatically. 'I'm just…learning new things about you.'

'Is that why you kissed me?' he challenged playfully, trying to lighten the mood and address the other hot topic. 'Because you realised I'm actually a nice guy?' Although trying to win her over or thinking about that kiss was trivial. They were going to be parents. That was the most important thing.

She shook her head and scoffed. 'We'll come to the kiss,' she said, deflecting. 'Let's get back to talking about the baby.'

'Right. So what are you going to say to Tris?' he asked. 'About the baby being mine and not his.'

Théo hated keeping secrets from his brother, but he'd been at the hospital until after midnight last night and Tris and Victor were busy today with last-minute wedding preparations. Plus it was Connie's place to tell him.

Connie shrugged and frowned. 'Just the truth, I

guess. I'm seeing him tonight. I thought it would be better to tell him in person so I can see if he's truly upset.' She nibbled at her lip. 'Do you think he will be?'

Before he'd even registered he'd moved he touched the back of her hand, drew her fingers through his. Her skin was warm and soft and he felt instantly closer to her, as if they would figure out this parenting journey together. 'I hope not. He was happy to help you out without wanting any parental responsibilities,' he reasoned. 'He must have prepared himself for the possibility that the procedure might not have worked. And it's not like there's ever been anything romantic between you two.'

'No,' Connie said, worry tightening her mouth as her fingers flexed against his. 'I just hope he isn't…disappointed.'

'I'll call him this evening to see how he feels,' Théo said, squeezing her hand. 'I'm sure he'll be happy for you and invested in last-minute wedding plans. Don't worry. We're in this together and we've already established that we both love Tris to bits.'

Connie's smile widened and lit her eyes. That zing of awareness arced between them once more. She didn't pull her hand away, so he stroked his fingertips over her skin. 'Is there anything you need from me?' he asked quietly. 'With regards to the baby and the pregnancy?'

He didn't want to crowd her, but he wanted her to know that he'd be there if she needed him.

'I don't think so.' She smiled. 'I've seen my family doctor and I'm booked in for a scan after Christmas. I can let you know the time and date if you'd like to attend.'

'Yes, I'll be there. Thank you.' He waited until she looked up then added, 'I realise this wasn't how you planned it and that it might seem that I'm muscling in on your pregnancy, the way I muscled in on your surgery that first day. But I don't want to take over. I just want to help and to have a chance at a relationship with our little one.'

She nodded, her eyes shining. 'Of course, Théo. You're its father.'

Relief washed through him. Until that moment he hadn't been certain that Connie would allow him access to their baby. But as a few beats of charged silence passed, a new kind of relentlessness built. Just because they were having a baby together hadn't diminished their chemistry. Not even the possibility that she would have Tris's baby had achieved that.

As if she too was aware of it, and wanted to take a step back, Connie slid her hand from his and picked up her mug, taking a sip.

Théo swallowed down the surge of panic and physical desire, the confusing feelings drowning out the urge to get to know Connie better, because she was going to be the mother of his child. They needed to stay on talking terms. There'd be plenty of time over the next nine months to get to know each other beyond what they knew from briefly being past lovers. Théo couldn't risk failing at another relationship and missing out on contact with his child. Anaïs and he had each played their part in the breakdown of the marriage and lack of clear communication, but Théo could admit his failings.

'So, about that kiss,' she said, when she placed her mug back down on the table. 'I've never denied our chemistry, but I was obviously feeling emotional last night. And it's Christmas...' She raised one shoulder in a shrug. 'I told you it makes people behave badly.'

There was mirth in her eyes, a small smile tugging at her lovely lips, so Théo smiled back, letting her off the hook.

'Right,' he said, slowly nodding. He understood why she would back-pedal. Things were complicated enough between them without adding sex to the mix, no matter how desperately and inconveniently tempting.

'I mean, clearly we're still attracted to each other,' she went on conversationally, as if they were discussing Christmas gift ideas. 'But we'd be foolish to do anything about it, don't you agree? It's like you said, the baby is the important thing.'

Unsure who she was trying to convince, him

or herself, he nodded. 'You're right—there are other priorities now.' But before yesterday, before he'd discovered Connie's baby was also his, he'd fantasised over and over about sleeping with her again, perhaps going on a few dates to see if there could be anything there worth pursuing now they were both in a better place emotionally.

She nodded, taking her cue from him. 'It's like you said, I've more or less written off dating anyway. And you've been through enough drama with your divorce. It's family that's important now. Creating one that meets everyone's needs.'

'I can't argue with any of that,' he said wistfully. The last thing he wanted to do was recklessly indulge his desires and risk upsetting or hurting Connie, given things were already so precariously balanced. He couldn't survive losing another person he loved and, even though his baby was little more than a ball of cells, he'd discovered that parental love was pretty much instantaneous.

'Of course,' she said carefully, glancing down at the table, 'I'm in no position to have sex with anyone else at the moment either. I mean, I'm having a baby. *Your* baby.'

'I'm aware of that,' he said, his stare holding hers as possessive feelings conjured up hypothetical men she might have otherwise slept with. But was she saying she'd thought about sleeping with him again too? That she'd been open to exploring their chemistry before the fateful call from the clinic had changed everything? That certainly explained the passion of last night's kiss.

Théo's heart thudded with pointless excitement. 'If it helps,' he said, his tone playful, 'I'm willing to abstain from sex until after the baby is born to keep you company.' With his head full of Connie and the baby, he'd have no appetite for dating let alone sleeping with anyone else anyway.

She laughed. 'Thanks. I appreciate the offer. I'll let you know if your sacrifice is necessary.'

Théo grinned, glad they were able to tease each other, given the tension of the past few days. 'So we just ignore the kiss? Ignore our chemistry?' he asked, certain that he could try but would probably fail. Hopefully focussing on Connie's pregnancy and the baby would help strengthen his resolve just enough.

She nodded. 'We just ignore it. I promise not to kiss you again.' She smiled, apology and a mischievous glint in her eye. 'Just don't go standing near any mistletoe.'

'Okay,' he said, laughing it off. 'Good decision.'

Although in reality there was no decision to make. The needs of baby trumped their own physical needs. As Anaïs had accused, Théo had a tendency to hold back emotionally. And Connie had some pretty big trust issues. They needed all their energy to ensure they could get along as parents.

'Friends, then,' he said, holding up his mug of

hot chocolate in a toast, somewhat reassured that this was for the best. He would make it work.

'Santé,' she said with a smile and clinked her mug to his.

But something about the way she looked at him as she sipped heated his blood and left him hungry for more, complications or not.

CHAPTER NINE

AFTER TRAIPSING THE streets of Paris's sixth arrondissement with Théo, and after their heartfelt talk over hot chocolate, all Connie truly wanted was to go home and process her up-and-down feelings. But she had another emotional conversation to get through. She needed to tell Tris the outcome of their botched plan.

Curled into her friend's comfy sofa, nursing a mug of steaming tea, Connie brushed aside the memory of Théo's exhilarating farewell embrace as he'd wished her luck and told her to call him any time if she needed to talk. Stalling for time, she glanced around Tris and Victor's cosy and chic apartment. It was decorated for Christmas with a stunning real pine tree in the window, garlands of fresh spruce, cedar and holly draped on the mantel and clusters of lit pillar candles nestled here and there to create a cosy ambience of flickering light.

'It's so stylish in here,' Connie said, unable to fight the magic of Christmas, despite her nerves and worries that Tris would be upset by her news. 'Can I borrow Victor to decorate my apartment?' she asked playfully of Tris's partner, who was one of Paris's most sought-after interior designers. 'I haven't put up a single decoration yet.'

'Of course you can,' Tris said, placing his drink on the coffee table. 'He'd jump at the chance.' He took a seat next to her wearing an encouraging smile. 'So tell me. Any news?'

His stare sparkled with hopeful excitement and Connie swallowed and set her tea aside, terrified to hurt his feelings. Part of her wished she'd brought Théo along for moral support.

Pulling herself together, she reached for his hand and nodded bravely. 'It worked, Tris. I'm pregnant.' Tears stung her eyes as he beamed and squeezed her fingers.

'Congratulations. I'm so happy for you, Con.' He dragged her into a comforting hug but she pulled back.

'Thanks.' She sniffed, her joy dampened by the clinic's mistake. 'But there's more. Please don't be upset.' She gripped his hand tighter, begging him with her eyes.

'Okay,' he said with a small frown that made Connie feel sick.

She took a deep breath. 'I found out yesterday that there was a mix-up at the clinic. I'm really sorry, Tris, but it turns out I wasn't actually given your specimen during the insemination procedure.'

'What? That's crazy.' His frown deepened. 'So whose specimen were you given?'

Connie swallowed, her throat dry. There was no way to sugar-coat it. 'Théo's.'

Tristan's mouth gaped in shock. 'My Théo?' he asked and Connie nodded in confirmation, her treacherous emotions forcing images of what a great father family-obsessed Théo would likely be into her mind.

'I don't understand...' Tris said, frowning. 'Why did they have Théo's sperm at the clinic?'

'Apparently it was an old sample,' Connie explained. 'He donated for money when he was a medical student. He said it was to buy you a gaming console for your eighteenth birthday.'

'Wow,' said Tris, looking stunned. 'I never knew that.'

'Are you disappointed? Angry?' she asked cautiously after a moment of searching his expression. 'It's okay if you are. I was. So was Théo.'

Tris shook his head. 'I'm surprised. I'm not sure how else I feel, but it's kind of irrelevant anyway. The deed is done. You're pregnant.'

'I'm sorry,' she said, gripping his hand tighter. 'It wasn't supposed to happen this way. You made a selfless gesture to help me and it all went wrong. I still feel frustrated with the clinic.' And confused for herself.

And for Théo…? She had too many feelings to untangle. She knew being his friend was for the best, but she wasn't sure how she would find the strength to resist temptation. Just spending time with him made her feel…alive.

Tris squeezed her fingers. 'Don't be sorry. The main reason I offered to donate was because I don't want children of my own. But I'm thrilled for you that it worked. That you're going to have the baby you wanted. What does Théo think about it all? He must be overjoyed. He's always wanted kids.'

Connie inhaled a shaky breath, recalling Théo's thrilling possessiveness, his offers of help and his eagerness to attend the antenatal scan. 'He was shocked too at first, obviously. But he says he wants to be involved so I'm just getting used to that idea.'

Tris tilted his head in understanding. 'Yes, I'm afraid he will want to be as hands-on as possible. He's always dreamed of having a family but after his marriage to Anaïs failed I guess he's really only dated casually since. How do you feel about sharing the baby when that wasn't part of your plan?'

Connie blinked away the sting in her eyes, grateful that, after the initial shock had worn off, Théo had been wonderfully supportive, saying all the right things. 'I was stunned and angry about the mix-up at first, obviously. I mean, I wouldn't have chosen to do it this way or with Théo.' She looked down at her lap, ashamed of her disloyalty and eager not to criticise Théo in front of Tris. 'But after time to get used to the idea, I think we can find a way to make it work. We have to.' Teamwork didn't seem so bad after all with a man like Théo.

Tris nodded and smiled. 'I think you can too. So does this mean you've decided to forgive him?'

'Of course. It was just a misunderstanding,' she said, embarrassed by her part in it. 'We rushed into sleeping together three years ago when neither of us was ready.'

Tris nodded and reached for her other hand. 'I know he hurt you back then, but Théo is an honourable guy. A great guy. You could do a lot worse for a baby daddy.'

Connie laughed then groaned, burying her face in her hands. 'Oh, Tris… What a mess. Part of me still can't believe it's all happening.'

Tris rubbed her back soothingly. 'At least you're still keeping it in the family. I'll still be Uncle Tris, although please never ask me to change a nappy. That might push our friendship a step too far.'

Connie looked up, her throat aching as she tried to smile through the sting of tears. 'You're really okay with this?'

'I'm really okay. I promise. But…what about

you and Théo and your, um, history?' Tris picked up his drink, sipped and settled back into the sofa.

'There is no me and Théo,' she said. But even as she denied it, she recalled how exhilarating it had felt when he'd touched her hand in the café earlier. Recalled that reckless, seriously sexy kiss outside the hospital that she'd started.

She parted her tingling lips, abuzz from just the memory of how much that kiss had turned her on at the time. If they'd been in a different location, if he hadn't been on call, would she have stopped at a kiss? Or would she have been swept up in their chemistry and slept with him again? Because despite what she'd said to him about ignoring their chemistry, she'd had to constantly stop herself from touching or kissing him again as they'd traipsed around the city.

'Really?' Tris pushed with a narrowed stare, perhaps sensing her fickle train of thought. 'Because I know that cagey look on your face.'

Afraid to answer Tris's question, she looked down at her lap. Now she and Théo had talked, they had their polite and mature guarantee to fall back on: to focus on being friends and parents. Surely that was enough incentive to keep temptation at bay.

'You're right,' she said finally, sighing. Who was she trying to kid? She needed to talk to someone. 'It's not going to be that cut and dried, because I kissed him last night outside the hospital when I was feeling emotionally overwhelmed.'

And what was more, despite her promises, she couldn't one hundred per cent swear that she wouldn't do it again. It was just so…tempting. And good. And now she'd added fresh memories to those of the past.

'Okay…' Tris held up his hand. 'No judgement here. I mean, you're obviously still hot for each other in spite of everything.'

Connie nodded, tired of denying it and secretly thrilled that Théo might be struggling too. They *were* crazy hot for each other. 'But we've talked about it,' she said, trying to convince herself that ignoring their chemistry was for the best, 'and we both agree to forget about that and focus on the baby. That's all that matters now, right?'

Not sure if she wanted Tris to agree with her or point out the glaringly obvious flaw in their plan, she looked up expectantly.

'Right,' Tris said, nodding, his expression full of worrying doubt. 'I mean, of course, there are other ways to deal with chemistry,' he went on, his stare suggestive. 'It's not like you haven't done it before. And neither of you is looking for a re-lationship.'

As if highly infectious, Tris's doubts made Connie's multiply. How would she see Théo every day, share her pregnancy with him and eventually her baby and not want him with the same mindless preoccupation? When she wasn't working, Théo, his heart-stopping smile, his mad sexual skills and how awesome that kiss had been were all she could think about.

'Are you encouraging me to have a fling with your brother?' she asked, her pulse leaping at the intoxicating idea. After all, they were adults. She wasn't interested in dating other men, given she was pregnant. Nor was it fair that they'd made a baby without any physical contact when they'd previously been great together in that department…

'Do you want to have a fling with my brother?' Tris asked, looking mildly uncomfortable but also daring her to be honest.

She might…

'Does he want to have one with you?' Tris continued when she didn't respond. 'I mean, you're both adults. Théo doesn't date much these days. And personally, I'm not sure how in the hell you've managed to last three years without sex.'

Connie playfully smacked his arm and dramatically flopped back against the cushions. 'I'm so confused. And hormonal. You have to help me figure this out. You're my friend.'

'No way.' Tris shook his head and scooted down the sofa, literally distancing himself. 'You're on your own with this decision. He's my brother.' He took a sip of his tea, then gave her the side eye and a cheeky wink.

They both cracked up and the conversation shifted to the wedding plans. But try as she might to force Théo from her mind, Connie found herself picking at the scab of the sensible, restrained decision they'd made over hot chocolate for the rest of the night.

CHAPTER TEN

Two weeks to Christmas

A WEEK LATER, Connie stood on the balcony of the Hôtel Marquis alongside the rest of the wedding guests, beaming at the camera. The boutique hotel in the heart of Paris where Tris and Victor had tied the knot boasted stunning views of the Eiffel Tower. As the wedding party posed for another group photo, Connie beamed, her cheeks aching because she'd smiled so much already. Tristan and Victor's winter wedding had been small, intimate and breathtakingly romantic. She'd shed more than one tear throughout the ceremony, her gaze repeatedly drawn to the man at Tristan's side, his handsome best man, Théo.

While the photographer adjusted his camera settings, Connie glanced over at her friend, who looked gorgeous in his royal-blue suit and so happy he wore a permanent smile. Théo, at his side, beamed with pride, his unwavering love and support of Tris almost bringing fresh tears to Connie's eyes.

Three years ago when they'd first met, she hadn't truly appreciated everything Théo must have done for his brother over the years. But seeing them together on this special day, knowing how Théo felt about family, highlighted the strength of their sibling bond. Théo was completely invested in Tris's happiness, as if it represented a safeguard from everything they'd been through growing up, losing not one but two maternal figures in short succession and never knowing their father. No wonder Théo was obsessed with the perfect family. No wonder he'd avoided the risk of falling in love and losing yet another person from his life after his marriage had failed. But he had so many great qualities, it hurt Connie's heart to think of him alone out of fear to be hurt again.

Blaming her hormones for the rush of longing and compassion she felt for the man she was learning something new about every day, Connie slapped on another smile as the camera clicked once more.

Leaving Tris and Victor to have couple shots, Connie stepped inside with the other guests, grateful to be out of the chill. Théo materialised before her with a glass of bubbles he assured her were zero alcohol. In a room full of other people, they were still drawn to each other.

'You look beautiful,' he said, passing her the glass, his stare brimming with admiration and heat as it passed over her body.

'Thanks,' she croaked, her skin tingling everywhere his stare rested so her breasts ached and heat pooled in her belly. 'So do you.'

Understatement of the century. Théo wore a tailored suit as an acrobat wore a full Lycra body leotard. The cut showed off his tall muscular physique, broad shoulders and confident grace. The dress shirt and tie gave him an additional air of authority he in no way needed and when he removed the jacket his backside in the dress trousers made her want to bite her own hand to hold in a lusty groan.

For the past week at work, they'd dodged all talk of the elephant in the room: their stifling chemistry, that crazy hot kiss and their plan to ignore both and just be friends. But escaping Théo seemed impossible. If anything, the decision to be friends had made her longing and obsession much worse. The urgency to feel something, anything, beyond this constant desire was overwhelming. She needed either to run away from Paris and her life to avoid him or stop denying herself and rip off his clothes.

She swallowed, covering the nervous gesture with a sip of virgin fizz, hoping to successfully dodge the near constant pull of his forcefield for a few more hours until she could escape.

'You look like a proud father,' she teased as they both watched the newly-weds pose for joyful photos backdropped by Paris's iconic landmark. Any subject was better than trying to untangle her conflicted feelings, how, ever since that night of the kiss, she'd thought about him as a dieter dreamed of chocolate cake.

And he hadn't made it easy on her. He'd sent her messages about antenatal classes and well-respected obstetricians. They had discussed Tris and his reaction to the news of the mix-up. And every time their eyes had met over a patient or the operating table, she'd felt it: a thrilling certainty that, whatever had happened in the past, this man cared about her. And it had been so long since she'd felt cared for.

'I am proud,' he said about Tris, his gorgeous eyes shining with the kind of emotion that made Connie choked. 'My brother is an incredible man and he deserves to be happy.'

'I can't argue with you there.' Connie nodded vigorously, certain she could say the same about Théo. 'As you know, I love him to bits.'

Théo smiled and Connie caught her breath, her next question slipping past her guard. 'What does happiness look like for you?'

Théo frowned at her directness. 'I guess it's this,' he said, glancing at Tris then back at Connie. 'Tris and Victor happily married and you and I raising our baby.'

Connie nodded, mildly disappointed by his answer. But of course, like Connie, Théo wasn't looking for love and she understood why. Except he too had so much more to give.

She glanced around the room, aware that most of the family members in attendance belonged to Victor's side of the family. 'So you and Tris were never tempted to find your father?' she asked hesitantly, desperate to talk about anything other than how much she wanted him, despite her denials, the complications and how dangerous it felt. 'Tris doesn't like to talk about it.'

'No,' Théo confirmed, looking down at his feet as if he too was reluctant. 'I have no real memories of him. Just a photograph of him holding me as a baby. He left when I was two, before Tristan was born.'

'Why do you think he left?'

Théo shrugged, his obvious discomfort building. 'Maman always used to say that he loved us but had no fixed abode when she'd met him, and he struggled with settling in Paris. That he needed to be free. I have no idea if that's true and somewhere in my angry teens, I stopped waiting for him to come and find us and rescue us from care. Instead, I tried to be the kind of big brother Tris could look up to'

'Théo…' Connie whispered, her heart aching for him so she touched his arm and squeezed.

'It's fine,' he said, brushing his moment of vulnerability aside. 'As youngsters we never felt like we missed out. We were raised by our wonderful *maman* and grandmother and had all the love and happiness a kid could need.'

He looked up and locked eyes with Connie. 'That's why I want our baby to feel the love of family, yours and mine, all around them.'

Connie nodded, momentarily too choked to speak.

Whenever he discussed his past, she'd noticed he focussed on the positives and on Tris. But now that she'd pushed him, Connie couldn't help but wonder if minimising his own grief and confusion was a defence mechanism. Drawn to him, and to his past heartache, Connie stepped closer and lowered her voice. 'Tris once told me your mother died in a car accident.'

Théo nodded, looking uncomfortable. 'I was eight and Tris was five,' he said hesitantly.

'What was your grandmother like?' she gently pushed, desperate to understand what was holding him back, sabotaging his marriage and stopping him from taking another chance on a relationship.

The intense look on his face, the few seconds of silence before he answered, wrapped them in a bubble of privacy. The noise of chatter and laughter and glassware clinking dimmed.

'Mémé was wonderful. Caring and fun. We lived with her until she got too sick to care for us,' he said unemotionally. 'She died of breast cancer four years after we lost Maman.' His voice was matter-of-fact but Connie felt every emotion and fear he must have felt back then as a scared twelve-year-old trying to put on a brave face for his little brother.

'I'm so sorry that happened to you.' She stepped closer and touched his arm again so her heart fluttered erratically and all she could think about was holding him, letting him know that he was no longer alone.

'Don't be,' he said, shrugging it off in a way that appeared well practised. 'Tris and I were two of the fortunate ones. We had each other. We were placed in the same foster home and always managed to stay together. Not every sibling in care is as lucky.'

Connie nodded, aware he was minimising his grief, which would have been every bit as confusing and terrifying as Tristan's, despite their three-year age gap. Twelve was no age to throw off childhood to care for the emotional well-being of a younger sibling.

'Tris said you became his guardian at eighteen,' she said, coaxing him to continue because she needed to understand him better. For herself and for their baby. 'That was a big responsibility to take on.'

No wonder Théo felt so protective of and paternal towards Tris, given his life experience. It explained the emotional caution he'd admitted had contributed to the breakdown of his marriage. Explained why he avoided the possible rejection and loss of serious relationships now. It was as he'd hinted that day over hot chocolate—love just wasn't worth the risk.

'Well, there was no way I intended to leave him after I'd aged out of the system.' He shrugged, once more glancing Tris's way. 'He'd lost enough people in his young life.'

Connie stilled, her breathing tight. Couldn't he see that he'd lost just as much as Tris, if not more because Tris at least had had a wonderful male role model in Théo?

'So had you,' she said carefully, cautious of digging too deeply but seeing through his nonchalance.

Three years ago, when she'd acted on lust and slept with him, she had been too wrapped up in her own feelings of hurt and betrayal to look beyond what she'd overheard that fateful morning. Now that they'd made a baby, they were bound together for life and she couldn't help but see the real man beneath the façade.

'He was a pretty good kid,' Théo said, staring outside where Tris and Victor still posed for photographs. 'I enrolled in university, got a part-time job and he was busy with school.' The quick flash of vulnerability on Théo's face as he shrugged made her throat tight. 'We made it work.'

Connie nodded, the hollow ache of longing inside her expanding as she saw him more clearly than ever. How many other young adults would be compelled to raise a teenaged brother? Théo was an exceptional man. Trustworthy, generous and inspiring. He would be a great father to their baby. Tris was right. Their child was incredibly lucky. Why did that make him even more dangerously attractive in her eyes? The man had been hard enough to resist when they were resentful past lovers.

'Have you told your family about the baby?' he asked, changing the subject, his eyes once more sliding down her body so she shuddered under a wave of spreading tingles.

Connie shook her head. 'Not yet. I wanted to wait until the second trimester before I tell them.'

He nodded. 'That makes sense.'

They stared at each other in loaded silence for a few seconds. Feeling closer to him than ever, Connie kept her feet glued to the floor, even though every bone in her body clamoured to step closer. 'How's your best man speech coming along?' she finally asked.

She too needed to change the subject before she threw herself into his arms and begged him to put her out of her self-induced misery with another passionate kiss.

'Good. I have plenty of funny anecdotes stored up here.' He tapped his temple and grinned. 'And I'm not sure Tris has ever met a person who doesn't instantly adore him. My audience are primed. Piece of cake.' He shrugged, playfully confident.

Connie joined him in laughing but inside her insides twisted in yearning. Both Augustin brothers were kind of irresistible, charismatic and charming. But there was only one who made Connie ache and burn, fearful for her sanity and ready to throw caution to the wind for one more dangerously reckless kiss.

As the evening party hit its stride, Théo looked up from his current conversation with a group of wedding guests, his eyes, as they'd been for most of the endless-seeming day, drawn to Connie across the room.

She looked achingly beautiful. Her navy-blue halter dress caressed her figure in way that tortured him with memories of her gorgeous body. Her long, tumbling dark hair kissed bare freckled shoulders every time she moved. Théo's lips tingled, desperate to brush over her skin, to taste her, lingering, savouring, drawing out that passion he recalled from three years ago as if it were yesterday.

He mentally snorted. So much for friends...

While he ignored the conversation swirling around him and stared like a fanatic, Connie laughed at something Victor said, swinging her hair over one bare shoulder and exposing her neck.

Still unsettled from the way she'd drawn him out earlier when she'd asked about his upbringing, and tightly wound with sexual frustration, Théo groaned silently and momentarily closed his eyes. He needed a distraction from this lust spiral and fast. Disgusted by his weakness for her, he took one last look. Then he would stop staring for the rest of the night, have a cold shower and try to ignore how every passing day deepened the torture.

In that very moment, she turned her head and glanced his way. Their gazes locked with searing eye contact the way they had all day through what felt like a million accidental looks. But they hadn't been accidental. And they were both kidding themselves if they thought they could simply ignore this preoccupation.

They stared for a few seconds as if daring the other to look away first. With his heart thumping and telling himself he shouldn't want her after they'd agreed to try friendship, Théo conceded and dropped his gaze, pretending to rejoin the group conversation.

Why was he fighting so hard to deny himself? As soon as he'd recovered from the shock that she was having his baby, he'd vowed he wouldn't hurt her. Vowed to protect their relationship as parents as fiercely as he would protect their child. But they were both adults. They understood that neither of them wanted a long-term romantic relationship. If they surrendered to what was becoming an untenable temptation, they could dispose with all this… pining and move on, this time without the misunderstanding of before.

Leaving the group conversation he'd half-heartedly participated in while simultaneously watching Connie like a hawk, he crossed the room in her direction. He'd deliberately forced himself to give her space to talk to other guests this evening, but he was done deluding himself.

'Want to dance?' he asked when he reached her and she and Victor looked his way.

She hesitated for the merest fraction of a second, then smiled up at him and held out her hand. 'Sure.'

Théo took her hand and led her to the dance floor, where other couples were slow-dancing as the band sang covers of popular love songs. He held her close, placed his other hand in the small of her back and moved them to the music, entranced by the scent of her perfume, the length of her eyelashes and her gloss-slicked lips as she smiled.

'Are you having a good time?' he asked, his pulse going crazy as if he were a teenager on a first date. But she felt way too good in his arms, her breasts brushing his shirt, her stare wide and vulnerable, her breath shallow as if she felt it too. This incessant need.

She nodded and sighed happily. 'It's been such

a lovely wedding. Tris is so happy. I'm having a great time. How about you?'

'It's been magical,' he agreed. 'But I have to be honest, I haven't been able to take my eyes off you, as hard as I've tried.'

Maybe because he knew she was carrying his child, she'd never looked more radiant. Her lips parted in a soft gasp, excitement glowing in her eyes.

'Théo…' she whispered imploringly but she didn't look away and her pulse fluttered excitedly in her neck as she pressed her body a little closer.

'I know we're supposed to be ignoring the way we make each other feel,' he said, unable to deny his feelings. 'But I wanted you to know that, for me, it's a constant struggle.'

She looked down, a flush to her cheeks. 'For me too,' she admitted softly, glancing back up so their eyes met once more and energising euphoria pounded through his system.

Théo slid his hand a fraction higher, his fingertips grazing the mink-soft bare skin between her shoulder blades. 'Are you staying at the hotel tonight?'

She looked up from his mouth and need all but choked him. Surely she felt this fever raging in him, felt the connection they had little hope of denying. The last thing he wanted to do was complicate things further or hurt Connie. But they were already pretty complicated as it was, and this infatuation seemed to be going nowhere. He would never hurt her and it was just sex, something they already knew they were good at.

'Yes.' Her fingers curved over his shoulder, gliding around the back of his neck where her fingertips brushed his skin. Her lips parted invitingly. 'You?'

Théo nodded, his gaze drawn to her mouth, his instincts demanding he kiss her and finish what they'd started that night at the hospital.

'I'm in room twenty-eight,' he said quietly. 'You could come to me or I'll come to you, when the party is over.' His heart thudded against his ribs, his muscles tense. But he was beyond caring that she might sense how badly he wanted her. The time for pretence was over.

The song came to an end too soon. Théo reluctantly released her, trying to dampen down the flare of desire making his mouth dry and his body tense.

'My room,' she said quietly as she dropped her hand from his shoulder, her palm skimming his chest, which was rising and falling with his rapid breaths. 'Room number sixteen.'

She held his stare for a moment then, with the barest hint of seductive knowing smile, she left the dance floor and sought out Tris, leaving Théo to count the minutes until the party and his best-man duties were over.

CHAPTER ELEVEN

DRESSED IN THE hotel's robe after a shower, Connie sat on the edge of the bed, her stomach knotted in a ball of nerves. She glanced at her phone to check the time, her eyes darting to the stubbornly silent door. She stood. Paced. Chewed at her lip. Her mind veered back and forth between flickers of doubt and raging impatience.

Where was he? Maybe this was a mistake. Maybe she should text him and tell him she'd changed her mind. Only that would be a lie. She knew that come Monday morning when she saw him at work, she would want him still. Perhaps this way, there on neutral territory, they could get this…obsession out of their systems and move on. She trusted Théo. Not with her heart, but enough to sleep with him again. Enough to know that neither of them would allow sex to get in the way of raising their child.

A quiet tap at the door sent her pulse soaring. She hurried to open it and quickly dragged Théo inside.

'I thought you'd changed your mind,' she said, frantically taking in his appearance. He'd removed his tie and suit jacket, but still wore his white dress shirt and suit trousers. With his top few shirt buttons undone to reveal a glimpse of dark chest hair, he looked so sexy she almost sobbed.

'No.' Théo cupped her face and tilted up her chin, his stare boring into hers. 'Have you changed yours?'

Too turned on to speak, Connie shook her head as his breath gusted over her tingling lips. If he didn't kiss her soon she was going to explode or melt. 'But I think we should establish some ground rules,' she croaked, finding some hidden reserves of strength to shield her battle-scarred heart.

'Okay.' He nodded, his fingers restlessly sliding into her hair and his stare caressing her mouth with hunger. 'I'm listening.'

'It's just sex,' she said, sliding her hands around his waist because he was too far away. 'We're not stupid. We both know what we want and it's not a relationship. We've agreed to focus on the baby. And this time, we have a very good reason to stay friends after it's over.'

Impressed with her mental restraint, she dragged in a shuddering breath.

'I agree and feel the same.' He nodded, his thumb tracing her lower lip so she sighed and parted her lips, the tip of her tongue brushing the pad of his thumb. 'I'm ashamed of how miserably I failed to ignore this.'

'I know, me too.' Connie sighed as his hands slid to her shoulders and down her arms. 'I blame my hormones,' she said, tilting her head back to give him access when he leaned in and kissed her neck, groaning as he inhaled deeply and slid his mouth to the sensitive place just below her earlobe.

'I have no such excuse,' he murmured, Connie's body temperature soaring with every delicious glide of his lips.

She slid her hands up his muscular back and pressed her body to his until her breasts brushed his hard chest and her knees almost buckled with lust.

Pulling back, he tightened his arms around her waist. 'I just want you and I'm tired of denying it. But I promise, I won't hurt you.'

'I want you too,' she said, her breath panting as she looked up at him and processed his words, her heart stalling as they prodded at her deepest fear. 'Kiss me, Théo.'

Instead of immediately obliging, Théo slowly slipped the belt of the robe free and slid it from her shoulders, staring at her nakedness, his eyes dark with desire and determination.

'I wish I could say I'd forgotten how beautiful you are,' he said, his voice a husky croak as his stare shifted over her body, prolonging the anticipation so Connie ached for him from head to toe. 'But I haven't.'

His hand caressed her throat, her chest, unhurriedly cupping one breast and zinging the nipple erect with a brush of his thumb.

'I want to see you too,' she said, impatiently reaching up to undo the buttons of his shirt, but before she was even halfway down he dragged her body flush with his, wrapped one arm around her waist, cupped her face with the other hand and slowly, intently, lowered his mouth to hers.

A groan rumbled in his chest as he slid his lips over hers, finally giving her what she craved. But unlike the kiss outside the hospital, which had been a cautious reaction to an emotional day, this was passion unleashed, pure and simple. And Théo took control.

Connie moaned too as he parted her lips and their tongues surged together, sliding and tasting, the euphoria sweeping her entire body up into a storm of sensation. Her pulse raged and she forgot to breathe. Tongues tangled, lips clung, teeth bumped and moans were swallowed as they fought to stay connected amidst the firestorm.

Connie tried to undress him but the minute she exposed another inch of warm tanned skin, she couldn't stop herself from caressing, from pressing her naked body close so his scent was left behind on her skin.

'Take your clothes off,' she demanded when he finally let her up for air. She tugged his shirt free of his waistband and undid his belt, eager to get her hands on the body that was hard and straining towards hers as if any distance was too great.

Within seconds he was naked too. They stood facing each other, panting hard, their eyes and hands roaming each other's bodies as they re-learned contours and dips and sensitive spots. But unlike three years ago, Connie was pretty certain they were both stone-cold sober and desperate to savour every second of the night.

Théo scooped his arm around her waist and ducked his head, laving his moist tongue over her nipple. 'Are you too sensitive?'

'No.' Connie moaned as he sucked a little harder, her knees buckling. Sliding her hand around his erection to stroke him in return, she smiled when he growled and backed her up towards the bed.

This time when they parted for breath, there was a new urgency in his expression. He pulled Connie down to lie at his side, his mouth returning to hers and his hand caressing her breast, her waist, her hip and finally between her legs where she burned for his touch.

'I fought it as long as I could,' he admitted, sighing over her parted lips as he stared down at her, his fingers sliding over her clit.

'Me too,' she said, gasping and parting her

thighs as he stroked her faster and she stared into his dark eyes swimming with desire. 'If you hadn't cracked tonight, I would have.'

Rather than smile, he dipped his head and captured her nipple in his mouth. Connie moaned and writhed against him, needing him closer. 'Théo…'

'Do you want me to use a condom?' he asked, brushing his lips over hers as if he couldn't keep his hands and mouth off her. As if he ached and burned every bit as much as Connie.

She shook her head, certain that Théo was responsible and into safe sex. 'I haven't slept with anyone else since you,' she whispered, swallowing that vulnerable feeling when he looked down at her in surprise.

But then his expression turned possessive, his hand still working between her legs as he watched her submit to pleasure. Because his fingers were gliding in a rhythm that made her moan and writhe under him, she dragged his lips back to hers and kissed him deeply, pressing her tongue against his, her wild kisses taking him from carefully in control to untamed and determined.

'Connie,' he groaned as she hooked one thigh over his hip and dragged him on top of her so his erection was crushed against her stomach and not at all where she wanted him.

But rather than rush ahead, Théo found some hidden depths of restraint. He shifted, held his weight on his braced arms and kissed a slow tortuous path over her chest, her abdomen, her inner thighs and finally her sex.

'Théo,' she gasped as he went down on her, his tongue wreaking havoc as effortlessly as his fingers had done.

He positioned her thighs over his shoulders and Connie gripped his hair as delicious electrifying sensation uncurled from her pelvis to every part of her body. Close to orgasm, she cried his name, then moaned louder in protest as he reared above her, leaning over her to kiss her once more. She clung to his lips with hers, gripped his shoulders, his hips and buttocks, parting her thighs to urge him inside her.

'Why did we fight this for so long?' he asked, finally joining them, skin to skin, his heart thundering against hers.

'I don't know,' she wailed, biting her lip against the pleasure of his possession and the reverent way his gaze shifted over her face and down her body to where they were joined.

Connie smiled and moaned, her heart beating so fast she felt dizzy as she wrapped her legs around his hips and he sank lower, his face fierce with the desire she remembered from before.

But she knew him so much better now. Knew he was a good man with a massive heart. Knew that he cared fiercely about the people in his life and that he would value Connie, as the mother of his child, no matter what.

'You feel so good,' he said, cupping her face to drag her mouth up to his as he moved his hips, making her gasp.

'So do you.' She panted, her hips jerking to meet his as he began to thrust faster, quickly shoving them into a tangle of sweaty limbs and grasping hands, of pants and moans and the safety net of their connection past and present.

'Come for me,' he said, his hand delving between their bodies to stroke her clit as his hips powered harder.

Connie nodded, her stare locked to his so she saw the moment he shrugged off the shackles of restraint and acted purely on animal instinct, his wildness for her matching the fire burning her up.

'Théo,' she cried as he dived to capture her nipple in his mouth.

He groaned, crushing her body in his arms as her orgasm stole her breath and strength and even her mind so all she could do was cling to him and ride through the scorching inferno to the other side.

Moments later, as they lay panting and staring at the ceiling, catching their breath, Connie rested her hand on his sweaty, hair-dusted chest.

'Is my memory playing tricks on me, or was that better than three years ago?' She smiled, her heart pounding, endorphins draining as the first flutters of doubt burned in her chest. How would she give up sex that good? How would she give up a physical relationship with Théo when there would be no escaping their connection? How would she see him every day, watch him love their child, and not want him still?

Théo placed his hand over hers, raising it to his mouth to press a kiss there. 'Do you know, I think it might have been.' Dragging her close so her head rested on his chest, he pressed a kiss to her forehead.

'What is it about Christmas?' she chuckled, trying to dismiss the trickle of anxiety chilling her blood.

'Blame it on the silly season, why don't you?' he said, his voice light and teasing.

Connie smiled but, inside, that growing sense of foreboding unfurled. She should make him leave, erect those *just sex* boundaries, even though she wasn't ready for the night to be over, having denied this for so long.

Focussed on his promise not to hurt her and her certainty that this fling was as safe as it could be, given their stance on relationships and what was at stake, Connie tangled her fingers with his when he reached for her hand and brushed aside her fears.

CHAPTER TWELVE

THE NEXT MORNING after a scant hour of sleep, Théo stumbled down to the hotel's dining room for breakfast with the newly-weds, his gut a restless ball of exhilaration and apprehension as he scanned the room for Connie.

He'd spent most of the night in her bed. The first time had seeped into a second and then a third and he just hadn't been able to bring himself to leave, despite the feeling that he should in order to stick to the rules. But he couldn't seem to get enough of her, having denied himself for weeks. Just before dawn, she'd roused him from an exhausted nap and kicked him out of her hotel room, sending him off with a kiss that left them both impressively breathless considering the orgasm count.

But once he was alone under the shower spray, away from the physical temptation of Connie, his mind had finally found space for doubts. Not regrets as such, just the niggle of fear that, by further complicating an already entangled situation, he was essentially operating blind. Never a good thing for a surgeon.

Now, reassured that he and Connie were smart enough to stick to the ground rules they'd voiced last night and put the baby first, he spied Tris and Victor and Victor's parents and joined them at their table.

'Morning, everyone,' he said, taking a seat at Tris's side and signalling the waiter to order strong black coffee.

'How are you feeling?' he asked the couple as Victor's parents went up to the breakfast buffet. 'Any hangovers to report?'

'I haven't danced so much in years,' Victor said, shooting Tris an indulgent loved-up smile that made Théo mildly envious.

'You disappeared right on the dot of midnight,' Tris said, watching Théo shrewdly as Victor joined his parents at the breakfast buffet. 'Like Cinderella worried her coach was about to become a pumpkin.'

'Sorry. Us old guys need our beauty sleep,' Théo said evasively. 'But I had a great night. Are you happy to be a married man?'

His stomach pinched with another twinge of envy. He'd once been in Tris's shoes, blissfully in love, certain that life was about to begin, eager to embrace his future as a husband and father, unaware of the heartache and disappointment ahead.

But weddings were always romantic. Théo

wasn't really eager to have what Tris and Victor had, knowing as he did how things could go so very wrong. Especially now there was Connie and their child on which to focus. Only, having spent the night with Connie, waking up with her naked and wrapped around him like a vine, knowing that as he held her, he also held their baby… It had left him unsettled, as if what he'd once craved—the love of his life, a family of his own, belonging—was once more within grasping distance. The last two out of those three things were, he guessed. And the first… Was that worth the risk now there was a good relationship with Connie and his child at stake?

'Of course.' Tris beamed. 'I'm ecstatic. I can't wait for our few days in Geneva.' He glanced over at Victor longingly. 'But don't worry. We wouldn't miss Christmas Eve.'

'Has Connie been down?' Théo asked, accepting his coffee from the staff member and talking a scalding sip to cover the yearning in his voice.

'Not yet,' Tris said. 'Oh, here she comes now.'

Théo turned to see Connie enter the dining room and spy their table. Wearing a pair of black jeans and a red sweater, she looked utterly breathtaking, her skin glowing, eyes bright and her hair swept up into a messy topknot so her neck was on display. Memories of kissing her there swamped him—the softness of her skin, the scent of her perfume, the way she'd moaned in delight and clung to him harder.

'Morning.' She leaned down and pressed her mouth to Tris's cheek then took the seat opposite Théo. Her face wore a bright smile, her gaze landing anywhere but on him, and those possessive urges he'd experienced since discovering she was having his baby resurfaced. Théo realised with a dry swallow of fear that he wanted her again.

Under the table, he slid his feet forward until their toes touched and she looked up.

'Morning, Théo,' she said politely, a split second of vulnerability in her stare before she turned to Tris. 'What a fabulous wedding. I still have a romance hangover.'

Tris smiled and reached across the table for Connie's hand. 'Well, so far,' Tris said smugly, 'I can highly recommend getting married.' He smiled softly at Connie, whose cheeks flushed. 'Don't write it off completely, will you? You never know who is just around the corner.'

Théo winced, jealousy a jab between his ribs and compassion for Connie, who'd once been engaged, a burn in his throat. He looked down at the table, unable to witness her discomfort at Tris's throwaway words. His brother was just happy and wanted to see his best friend the same. He wasn't being flippant and obviously had no idea that Théo and Connie had restarted their physical relationship last night. But the idea of Connie one day moving on, of her maybe falling in love, of another man raising his child…completely decimated his appetite.

'Tea, please,' Connie said to the server during the tense moment that followed. Her stare avoided Théo as she added, 'I'm starving. Think I'll help myself to breakfast.' She stood and approached the buffet.

Tris turned accusing eyes on Théo. 'You slept with her again, didn't you?' he whispered harshly.

'Shh,' Théo urged. 'None of your business.' He pushed back his chair and stood but Tris gripped his arm.

'Be careful,' his brother urged, wearing a frown. 'Don't hurt her.'

Théo nodded, suddenly desperate to speak to Connie alone. 'I'm going to get some breakfast.'

At the omelette station, where the chef was busy cracking eggs for her order, Théo grabbed a plate and sidled close to Connie's side. Tris's words rang in his head. But hurting Connie was the last thing he wanted to do.

'How are you feeling?' he asked, carefully, after her abrupt departure from the table.

'Fine,' she said automatically, looking up at him with vulnerable eyes bearing a flicker of hurt. 'Did you tell Tris…? About last night? About us?'

'Of course not.' Théo frowned, horrified and a little depressed that she'd needed to ask. She clearly still had trust issues with him in spite of how close they'd grown this past couple of weeks.

With frustration coiling in his belly like an angry snake, he inched closer, wishing they were somewhere private so he could kiss her and hold her and reassure her that nothing had changed. 'It's our business, Connie. Tris is just on a high after yesterday and thinks everyone should be as in love as he is.'

'Thank you.' Connie nodded, looking both relieved and uncomfortable at the same time. 'Perhaps we just keep it to ourselves. Things are… complicated enough as it is. And it doesn't mean anything. We don't want Tris getting the wrong idea.'

'Of course not,' Théo said, a pinch of disappointment stealing his breath for a second. She was right about the complications. Last night he'd hoped that sleeping with her again would relieve the tension and allow him to think about something else, but he already knew that he wanted another night, and another… Dangerous wants he would need to contain.

Weighed down by apprehension, he dropped his voice. 'Are you having regrets?'

His pulse buzzed in his fingertips as if he'd stuck them into an electrical socket. He'd be lying if he said he hadn't had one or two doubts himself since leaving her room. But it was nothing he couldn't handle and set aside. He'd thought it all through in the shower. He would stick to the rules, enjoy a passionate fling with Connie until it had run its course, then he would make the switch to a friend, cherish her as a co-parent and do his best to never let her or their baby down.

Connie shook her head, a small frown tugging down her mouth. 'I mean, I think we need to be careful,' she said, glancing over her shoulder to the rest of the wedding party, who were tucking into their breakfasts and talking animatedly. 'But we're responsible adults. We went in with our eyes open.'

Théo nodded, desperate to touch her again. 'I was thinking the same thing,' he said trying to reassure her and himself. 'We can't afford to mess this up or mess each other around. There's more at stake this time than just the two us.' He glanced down at her stomach, knowing she would understand that his priorities matched hers.

'I agree,' she said quietly, a cautious smile spreading.

'That being said—' He inched closer still because he couldn't help himself, breathing in her subtle scent as visions of her naked and plastered against him surfaced. 'I wondered if you had plans later. I could make you dinner.' Cooking her meal could be classified as simply caring for her during the pregnancy so wasn't technically breaking any rules.

She inhaled a shaky breath but grinned wider.

'Because we don't see enough of each other every day at work?'

Théo shrugged and smiled back, his heart leaping with anticipation as the chef slid Connie's mushroom omelette onto her plate and added a sprinkle of chives with a flourish.

'I need to do some Christmas shopping later,' she said, talking her plate. 'I haven't even begun yet and it's less than two weeks until Christmas.'

Théo grinned. 'I could go shopping. It's a well-known fact that I am the official Christmas gift master. Just ask Tris.'

Connie chuckled and gave him a playful shove. 'The gift master? Self-proclaimed, I take it.'

Glad he could make her smile after that bumpy moment, Théo shrugged. 'Just think, next year, I can really go to town. Our little one's first Christmas is going to be so special.'

As if he'd dropped to one knee and proposed or announced to the entire room that they were a couple, the atmosphere chilled as Connie smiled thinly then looked away.

'Can I let you know about the shopping expedition? I might be too tired, although I really need to get it done.'

'Of course,' he said with a guilty wince. He was getting ahead of himself, dreaming of next Christmas when this one was yet to come. And Connie had planned to raise their baby alone.

With them sleeping together again she probably thought he was rushing ahead.

'Either way,' he said, 'the offer of dinner still stands.'

'I'll text you later.' With a small enigmatic smile, she took her breakfast back to their table, leaving Théo unnerved and in no way hungry for food.

He needed to be careful and temper his excitement for the baby. Ensure that his feelings about the pregnancy didn't spill over into his relationship with Connie. He didn't want to scare her off or further complicate their situation or break the rules. Nor could he make her any promises and risk another failure. Already the line he would need to walk seemed incredibly fine, as if one wrong move could ruin everything.

CHAPTER THIRTEEN

GALERIES LAFAYETTE, PARIS'S LARGEST department store, stocked everything on Connie's gift list. As she waited outside for Théo later that afternoon, memories of the night before pushed insistently at her mind.

If she'd thought she and Théo had been sexually attuned three years ago, the intervening time had only stoked the fire. A big part of her hadn't wanted the night to end. But the minute she'd closed the door on him that morning, her reservations had grown, stumbling over each other to make themselves known.

If they'd met years earlier, before his divorce and Guy's betrayal, Théo might have been the perfect man. He was everything she'd once thought she wanted in a partner: kind, dependable, honest and principled, with a great career. But he was also uninterested in giving love a second chance and she understood his reasons why. She even shared his reservations.

The horrified look on his face when Tris had

recommended marriage haunted her still. But she shouldn't have been surprised by his reaction and, no matter how right she'd felt in his arms, she was in no way ready for feelings or to be that vulnerable with another man. It wasn't worth the risk to her heart, especially when she and Théo had to work together and raise a child together, and he clearly felt the same.

Wishing she'd been able to refuse when he'd suggested shopping and dinner, she glanced up in time to see him appear from around the corner and cross the street. His smiling gaze caught hers, sending her blood pressure through the roof with dizzying excitement. So much for playing it cool and being careful.

He kissed both her cheeks in greeting then reached for her hand as they entered the store. Connie shuddered ridiculously at the intimacy of holding his hand. The man had kissed and tongued every inch of her body last night, possessing her until she'd sobbed his name, over and over again. She could still feel him between her legs when she walked.

But whereas Théo might be able to detach physical intimacy from emotional intimacy, Connie considered holding hands something that couples did.

'Did the newly-weds get off on their honeymoon okay?' she asked, because Théo was looking at her as though he wanted to devour her. *Again.* And she needed to think about something else.

'They did. I dropped them at the airport. They're excited to go skiing and visit the ice caves.'

Connie smiled. Tris's happiness was infectious and the wedding had certainly stirred up emotions for Connie. She couldn't help but wonder how different her life might have been if Guy had stayed faithful. But then she was also increasingly relieved that she was having Théo's baby, because she had no doubt he'd be a wonderfully dedicated father.

'Right, let's get this over with,' Connie said, sliding her hand from his and ambling towards the menswear department, determined to set aside the turmoil the events of yesterday had aroused.

While she considered a green cashmere sweater that Tris would love, Théo cautiously asked, 'You seem distracted. Are you upset…? About what Tris said earlier? You know he adores you and didn't mean anything by his comments about marriage. He just wants you to be happy.'

'I know,' Connie said, pretending to consider the same jumper in blue to hide her eyes from him. 'Don't worry. He's listened to me rant often enough to know that I won't be following him down the aisle any time soon. I think the green

for Tris, don't you?' she asked, holding up both
choices although she'd already decided.

Théo nodded, his frown deepening. 'Not all
men are the same,' he said quietly, forcing Connie into a defensive position.

'I know.' She still felt a little guilty for asking
Théo if he'd told Tris they'd slept together again.
But for Connie it was a sign that, no matter how
amazing last night had been, she clearly wasn't
ready to fully trust someone else.

'Do you think one day you'll be ready to move
on?' Théo asked, casually, as if he weren't really
interested in the answer.

'I don't know.' Connie replaced the blue sweater
and tossed the green one into her basket, her guard
rising. 'But it's like Tris said, never say never.'

Théo swallowed and hesitated as if considering his response while also debating dropping
the subject. Connie wished he would, but then
maybe it was better that he understood her stand-
point. Just because they'd slept together, nothing
had changed.

'I think Tris probably worries that you're
missing out on the potential of something good
because of your past,' he went on, looking increasingly uncomfortable.

'So are you,' she pointed out, turning the tables.
'You're just as reluctant to risk another failed relationship. We're both scared and with good reason, I think.'

Théo glanced down at the ground. 'You're right. It does feel safer to hold back. Having messed up before, I'm not sure I'm fit for romantic relationships.'

'And I'm not sure I can be that vulnerable again,' she said boldly, meeting his cagey stare. 'I'm certainly not interested in ever being as gullible as I once was. The way I look at it, I've had my one lucky escape.'

His dark eyes turned stormy as if he were jealous. 'Believe me, I'm not encouraging you to rush out and date other men. We're both committed to focussing on the baby for now.'

'Exactly,' Connie said, triumphantly, trying to rein in her touchiness and the hollow feeling of doubt that took her by surprise. He wasn't jealous, he was thinking about their child.

'I just want you to be happy,' he said, adding to Connie's doubts. He wanted her to be happy, just not with him.

Hardening her resolve to protect herself, she said, 'Rest assured that for the foreseeable future, you will be the only man in our baby's life.'

Tris was right. She needed to keep an open mind. Maybe one day she would be ready to find love again.

Leaving him at the sweaters, she shifted to a display of silk ties. Her heart pounded with adrenaline as she focussed on the selection and tried to block out his confusing words. He was obviously worried about his place in their child's life. And Connie could understand. She wouldn't want to miss a Christmas or birthday either.

Immediately spotting a tie that would suit Théo, she forced herself to ignore that one and chose another for Tris, adding it to her basket.

As she tried to calm down, she considered that she shouldn't have slept with him again. In indulging her desires, she'd opened herself up to doubts, second-guessing the decision and every word he said. She knew with absolute certainty that she would make the same choice to sleep with him again, but she was scared to trust her instincts. Hoping she was simply having a fatigue-induced wobble after a romantic weekend, she took some deep breaths.

Her skin prickled as Théo once more stepped close to her side, warming her with his body heat and turning her on with the scent of his cologne.

'This one is nice,' he said, reaching for her hand again and fingering the very tie she'd have chosen for him were she buying him a gift.

She hadn't planned on that. But maybe she should get him something, especially if she intended to attend his Christmas Eve party.

She plastered on a carefree smile and they moved on to the gift department, where Connie chose an interior design book for Victor and gifts for both her brothers and sisters-in-law. Finally, as they ended up in the children's department, she consulted her list.

'I have a horde of nieces and nephews to buy for,' she said, wandering over to a rack of toddler clothes, the cute little outfits building her excitement to meet their baby.

'What about this teddy bear?' Théo suggested, holding it up and waving its paw at Connie. 'Every kid needs a bear to love.'

Connie looked up and wrinkled her nose, her pulse flying at how sexy he was. 'Nolan is eight months old. I think his parents would appreciate a more useful gift.' She waggled a jumper-and-jeans set his way.

Théo gasped in mock horror and covered the ears of the teddy bear. 'She doesn't mean that,' he stage-whispered to the cuddly toy. 'She thinks you're very handsome and loveable.' Then to Connie he added, 'Look, he even has a festive bow tie. Take it from the gift master, we can't possibly leave him behind.'

Desperate to kiss him, Connie instead heaved an exaggerated sigh. 'Fine. But I'm getting the outfit too.'

Théo smugly tossed the bear into the basket and they moved on to boardgames for her older nieces and nephews.

'Are you going to be like this with our child?' Connie asked, distractedly, to take her mind off how badly she wanted him and how careful she needed to be, given he was so practised at holding back emotionally. 'Spoiling it to death.' She shot him a censorious look and then perused the selection of games lining one wall.

When he'd mentioned buying gifts for their child earlier that morning, she'd had a moment's panic. She understood and loved Théo's enthusiasm of fatherhood, but she simply couldn't think that far ahead, not now that she'd surrendered to temptation and slept with him again. Not when her feelings were so volatile and couldn't be trusted. It all felt too...permanent, which she guessed it was. She and Théo would always have a relationship as parents, just not a romantic one.

While her heart raced and her stomach pinched with fear that she might not be able to stick to the rules, Théo leaned down to press a kiss to her temple. 'Can you really spoil a child?' he said quietly, falling serious. 'Don't they simply need as much love and support and reassurance as you're able to give?'

Connie swallowed, her heart in her throat as she looked up at his earnest expression. He was going to be such an amazing father. And as he'd never known his own, as he'd lost both his female caregivers at a young age, Connie knew she would never be able to deny him a single indulgence. Even if it meant tolerating his extravagances and spending every Christmas with him and their child.

'I suppose you're right,' she croaked through her fear.

How would she spend so much time with him and still switch off this longing? How would she see him be the wonderful father she knew he would be and not want him for herself, for the connection that at times last night had felt so effortless and uplifting and right?

'Okay,' she said, swallowing down the hot ache in her throat that came whenever she imagined a young Théo trying to make sense of the loved ones he'd lost. 'I'm getting these two.' She pulled the boardgames from the shelf and placed them in the basket. 'I think we're done.'

They headed for the sales desk, where Théo insisted on paying for the Christmas bear he christened Claude. As she watched him charm the sales clerk with his handsome smile and good manners, Connie sighed with a confusing mix of unease and longing.

Maybe he was right. Maybe, one day, she might be ready to fall in love again. Maybe she'd find another man as wonderful and sexy and unselfish as Théo. Or maybe he was one of a kind and Connie would simply need to find a way to live with her regrets that she just couldn't have it all.

After an afternoon of shopping, they took a taxi back to Théo's apartment. Théo set the oven timer and put dinner in to warm and then carried in a tray of no-alcohol mulled wine to the coffee table before the fire, where Connie sat placing her purchases in the stylish, reusable fabric gift bags she'd bought at Galeries Lafayette.

'I love your tree,' Connie said, tucking her legs up beside her on the sofa, looking more relaxed than earlier, when she'd seemed distant and cagey as if, despite her reassurances, she did regret the night before.

Théo tried to calm himself, his sense of foreboding building. On the one hand, as he'd stated earlier, he too wanted Connie to be happy. He wanted her to let go of the past, to open her heart and stop punishing herself for what her ex had done. But on the other hand, he selfishly wanted her for himself. He certainly wanted to be the only important man in his child's life. And Connie's vagueness over the baby was making him feel paranoid.

But she was right. They were both messed up, both scared to take another risk when it came to relationships. And while she was content to mess around with him, at least he could feel secure that their priorities were aligned: work, each other, the baby.

That had to be enough.

'Victor helped me decorate it,' he said about the tree, sliding in next to her and resting his arm along the back of the sofa, because it had been too long since he'd touched her and his doubts were back. The worst one that, one day, Connie would move on and another man might help raise his child.

Brushing aside that terrifying thought, Théo focussed on keeping Connie relaxed. 'He and Tris have decided to go to Château Bijou a few days early,' he said, panic an acidic burn in his throat. 'To decorate the house for Christmas, for which I'm very grateful.'

'How many people have you invited to the *réveillon*?' she asked taking a sip of the warm spicy drink and sighing contentedly.

'Around ten. Just close friends and partners. Plus me, Tris and Victor and you if you decide to join us. Maybe next year you can decide whether we host here in Paris or at the *château*. Will you… bring the baby?' he asked, hesitant to upset her again as he slid his fingers to the nape of her neck to stroke her skin.

Her earlier reaction to his mention of the baby's first Christmas had plagued him all day. Yes, she'd originally planned to raise a child independently, but her evasiveness was worrying, fuelling his paranoia that he would mess things up between them and lose the most amazing gift he'd ever been granted.

'I…um… I guess so,' she said, staring at the fire. 'Although I'm pretty sure that babies aren't that into parties.' She glanced down at her lap and a disheartened burn began in his chest.

'Then I won't organise a party next year,' he said, resolute, trying to show her that she and their child were his priority. 'I'll just spend Christmas with you and our little one. Unless you have other plans, of course...'

The desperation in his voice scared him as much as the strength of his apprehension. He understood her emotional caution because he shared it. Yes, they'd complicated things by sleeping together again, but there was no way Théo would allow that, or anything else for that matter, to interfere with their role as parents.

'We can decide nearer the time,' Connie said, but wouldn't look at him.

Théo cupped her face and turned her eyes to his. 'Am I going too fast?' he asked quietly, the anxiety-driven burn behind his sternum spreading so he almost couldn't breathe.

'A little,' she said, smiling guiltily.

'I'm sorry,' he whispered, feeling as if he'd just stepped onto paper-thin ice covering the deepest part of the ocean. 'What I'm actually trying to say is that I don't care about parties. This relationship—you and me as parents—is the most important one of my life. And with the scan booked, I guess I'm feeling a bit overexcited about the baby.'

She smiled indulgently, resting her cheek on his arm and looking at him through her lashes. 'Me too. I just haven't really given solo parenthood a lot of thought yet. I'm not even sure how it's all going to work out. Shared custody, working, childcare… I guess by next Christmas I'll likely still be on maternity leave though.'

Théo held his breath, his heart racing with panic because he felt as if she was slipping away. 'I know this wasn't how you planned parenthood,' he said carefully. 'You thought you'd be doing it alone. But I want to be involved, Connie. I want to help if you need it and spend time with you and the baby. I think we can figure out all the details together. Just know that I'm here and willing.'

'I know and I appreciate that,' she said, her eyes shining as they moved over his face. 'I understand. Family *is* important. And you're right. Together we'll make our unconventional little family, just the three of us, work.'

Looking at him as if he were made of glass, she put down her glass and slid closer into his arms. Sagging with relief, he held her close, breathing through her hair as she rested her cheek over the thump of his nervously pounding heart. When she was in his arms like this, he felt invincible. But then the moment he tried to figure out the future, to plan and dream and visualise them being just friends, it all seemed insurmountable. After all, he'd failed to hold onto Anaïs and they'd been husband and wife. What if he somehow failed Connie and lost her and his baby too? He couldn't allow that to happen.

'Was it truly awful?' she whispered after a moment, looking up at him with shining eyes. 'I keep picturing you and Tris as scared little boys living with strangers and my heart breaks for you.'

Théo swallowed down the surge of desire for her as he registered her abrupt change of subject. Confused and reluctant to look back to the worst time of his life, he shook his head.

'No. Not awful at all,' he said, slipping straight into his favourite coping mechanism: denial. 'I don't really like to think about it. To talk about it. But we always had food and warmth and a safe place to sleep,' he went on, trying not to think about the nights he'd spent lying awake with tears soaking into his pillow. 'Just not a lot of love. At least not the kind of love we'd been used to.'

'I'm so sorry, Théo.' She pressed her lips to his as if she could kiss away his pain and grief. She pulled back, her stare searching his as if she easily saw the truth: that of course he'd been lonely and terrified and had needed to grow up pretty quickly to put on a brave face for Tris.

'It's fine,' he said, trying to smile while the past and his present desire for her collided in a sickening mass of renewed doubt. 'Our foster parents were good people but we weren't their real kids.'

Connie tilted her head with compassion. 'And you were old enough to know the difference, to remember your mother's and grandmother's love,' she said, intuitively understanding because she was a wonderfully caring woman. 'Tris was so lucky to have you.'

Théo's hands gripped hers tighter. He shrugged, his throat choked by fear. Fear that she would see how broken he was. That she too would reject and leave him, because his best wasn't good enough. That he'd be alone once more.

Connie cupped his face and peered into his eyes intently. 'But you were loved, Théo. By Tris, by your mother and grandmother. Even by your professor mentor, the one who left you the *château*. You had so much love, despite how much you lost, and because of the man you are, you still do.'

Because her words felt dangerous, painful, he wrapped his arms around her waist and dragged her close, kissing her until she moaned and twisted free, panting.

'Connie,' he said in warning, scared that she would demand he face all the feelings he'd buried all those years ago.

She gripped his face and forced him to meet her stare. 'Just like you want me to be happy, I want the same for you. Don't shut yourself off because a part of you maybe didn't process your childhood grief at the time. I know it's scary to put yourself out there, but maybe we both need to risk it again. One day, I mean.'

He frowned in denial, his heart racing because she saw something in him no one else ever had.

'I'm trying,' he said in desperation. 'Which is why I'm so excited about the baby. You don't understand what an amazing gift this is for me. If you let me, I'll cherish the two of you, always.' And part of him, that selfish part that wanted Connie for himself, would hate to see her happy with another man.

Connie blinked rapidly as if she might cry. 'I know you will. And what's more our baby is going to adore you and not because you're the gift master. But because you're its father and you're going to be so amazing.'

Overcome with feelings too big for his body, Théo crushed her in his arms. Her fingers glided through his hair as she held his face and kissed him with the same passion and need as the night before.

Théo groaned, not certain how he could want her again with the same urgency, as if last night hadn't happened. But with his emotions too convoluted to untangle, he was done questioning this.

Connie pulled back, then straddled his lap, shifting her hips forward until his erection was bathed in the heat between her legs as she kissed his lips, his face, the side of his neck. Théo slid his hands along her thighs, caressed her waist, her back, her shoulders, cupping her face to hold her lips to his as, finally, his panic that he might lose her receded.

'I want you,' she said, tugging at his sweater,

pulling it over his head then tossing it to slide her hands over his bare chest while she trailed her lips down the side of his neck.

Drunk with desire, he pulled back to stare into her beautiful eyes. 'You have to promise me that we won't allow anything or anyone to threaten our family,' he croaked, choked once more by fear that everything he had might be snatched away.

Deep down, he knew the biggest threat to his happiness was himself. He was terrified that he'd mess up again, let Connie and the baby down or somehow lose them for ever.

Connie shook her head, brushing her lips over his. 'I promise,' she said, impassioned. 'We are going to raise our baby together. You and me.'

He nodded, part appeased, part sensing that she was still holding back. And he couldn't blame her. They were both damaged, both navigating an unplanned situation, both desperate not to hurt each other.

As he crushed her close, his paranoia rose up. He needed her to understand that he was trying his best. 'You can trust me, Connie. I want you to know that. I won't let you down.'

'I do trust you and I know.' She nodded so he was engulfed by relief, relief that was then dampened when she added, 'But, please…don't ever make me a promise that you can't deliver.'

Théo stared deep into her eyes, his confusion once more building at her warning. But she was right to be cautious. Better to value what they already had than to try for something more and fail.

'I won't.' Théo swore, determined to double down on his efforts to focus on the baby and on not hurting Connie. All that mattered were the promises they'd made and how she made him feel in that moment.

As she trailed her mouth over his chest, scooting back on his lap, his mind all but blanked as arousal overwhelmed him. Chasing the same blind desire they'd surrendered to last night, Théo kissed her, pausing only to remove her sweater and pop her bra clasp while she attacked the fly of his jeans. In seconds they were naked, their caresses, kisses and groans finally shoving his doubts aside.

As he buried himself inside her and drove them towards climax, he renewed his vows to take extreme care, to shut down any dangerous flights of fancy about having more of her than this, and to simply value what he'd always craved and what was tantalisingly tangible: family.

CHAPTER FOURTEEN

IT WAS THE Wednesday after Tris and Victor's wedding before Connie and Théo were back in Theatre together again. Since that endlessly romantic weekend, they'd seen each other every day. Snatching a coffee together during the work day, speaking on the phone, knocking on each other's apartment doors late at night for the wild, uninhibited sex neither of them seemed able to do without.

Despite the promises they'd whispered to each other Sunday evening on the sofa before the fire in Théo's apartment, with every passing day, Connie grew increasingly aware of two things: One, she was scarily addicted to Théo, and two, he still seemed intent on emotionally distancing himself. He was playful and attentive, as crazy for their intimacies as her and said all the right things. But whenever the conversation steered anywhere near his past or his feelings, he subtly changed the subject. Connie couldn't blame him. Of course, she was trying to do the same thing, reluctant to trust what was going on inside her head and heart.

Meeting up with him in the anaesthetic room off theatre three, Connie smiled politely his way while her heart raced, just from his friendly glance.

'Good morning, Mrs Pascal,' Connie said to their seventy-seven-year-old patient. 'Are you ready to be a new woman?'

Marjorie Pascal had presented with slowly progressive weakness of her legs, an unsteady gait and back pain. The diagnosis—a spinal meningioma—was a benign tumour of the membrane covering the spinal cord. Hopefully removing it would alleviate all her symptoms.

'I'm in good hands with you two,' Marjorie said, fondly reaching for Théo's hand and gazing up at him with adoration.

Connie smiled and concealed a shudder. Sadly, she shared Marjorie's adoration. But the emotional turmoil raging inside her contrasted harshly with the warning bells that had been going off in her head for days. If Théo was guarding his emotions the way he'd always done, she needed to do the same or she might end up hurt.

'We'll see you when it's all over,' she told the elderly woman who was the main carer for her husband who suffered from dementia. Marjorie had confided in Connie that they were about to celebrate their fiftieth wedding anniversary. Some people really did find their soul mate and spend their lives together.

She tugged her mask over her face, and Théo joined her in the scrub room, the sense of déjà vu stifling. Was it only a few short weeks ago that he'd joined the team at St Raphaël? Then they'd been hostile strangers and now they were having a baby and a physical relationship, sharing every aspect of their lives together as if making a life-long commitment to each other.

As they scrubbed up side by side, they discussed the technical aspects of the surgery, which involved removing the spinous processes of two of the vertebrae to access the tumour, resection of the mass, followed by closure of the defect in the dura, the membrane covering the spinal cord, with a synthetic patch. At a pause in the conversation, Connie's mind turned to Christmas.

'I meant to say,' she added as they each scrubbed their hands, 'I will join you for Christmas Eve if the invitation still stands.'

Although part of her was dreading spending Christmas in Provence. No matter how often she chastised herself to be careful or reminded herself that Théo wasn't interested in a real relationship and she was still terrified to be hurt again, she couldn't seem to get enough of him, craving his company and his touch, as if she were already falling helplessly in love.

But she couldn't go there. Yes, she'd come to

trust him to some degree. But how could she give him her heart when they were both scared to take that final leap of faith? When he wasn't sure he could make another romantic relationship work and she was scared to trust her instincts and confess that she was developing feelings. When there was one very good reason to be cautious and hold back: the baby.

'That's great,' he said, smiling her way. 'Tris will be delighted and so am I. We can take the train down to Marseilles together on the twenty-fourth if you like.'

Connie nodded, desperate not to interpret his excitement as anything more than his desire to play festive happy families. They stepped into the operating room to gown up and soon the surgery was under way and all thoughts of Christmas and their relationship were sidelined.

The slow, cautious surgery was almost complete, when the cardiac-monitor alarms sounded and the anaesthetist shot to his feet.

'She's in ventricular tachycardia,' he said. 'Blood pressure falling.'

Connie and Théo and the anaesthetist all felt for a pulse.

'Nothing,' Connie said, glancing up at Théo, who also shook his head.

Abandoning the surgery, Théo commenced cardiac compressions on Marjorie while Connie readied the defibrillator to shock the heart back into a regular rhythm and the anaesthetist stuck gel pads onto the patient's chest.

With the first shock administered, all eyes glued to the cardiac monitor, a collective sigh of frustration seeming to sound as the heart showed zero response.

'Still no pulse. Administering adrenaline,' the anaesthetist said as Théo recommenced chest compressions.

They repeated the defibrillation-CPR cycle three more times, growing increasingly desperate with each cycle as the patient remained stubbornly in cardiac arrest.

'Keep going,' Connie pleaded, her stare clinging to Théo's as if he could miraculously fix this.

Connie couldn't bear to consider the consequences of losing this patient, who until this surgery for a debilitating but otherwise benign condition was fit and healthy.

'She takes care of her husband,' Théo explained to the anaesthetist and theatre nurses, who were looking increasingly pessimistic as time went on. 'They're about to celebrate fifty years together.'

Connie swallowed, sharing Théo's desperation and loving that he too knew these relevant facts about Marjorie. Losing a patient was always hard. Losing one after what should have been a straightforward surgery the week before Christmas would be devastating.

Seeing that Théo shared her determination,

Connie recharged the defibrillator paddles, ready to deliver the next shock.

'Clear,' Théo said, holding up his hands, his shocked, grave stare urging Connie to proceed.

This time with the shock delivered, the heart rhythm returned to normal. Shaking from adrenaline and relief, Connie felt for a pulse, nodding as the artery beat steadily at her fingertips.

'Blood pressure climbing,' the anaesthetist said.

But Connie could only look to Théo, her heart in her throat with gratitude and euphoria that together they'd managed to revive their patient.

As the anaesthetist drew Marjorie's blood for testing and handed it to a theatre technician, Connie focussed on completing the surgery and sewing up the patient's wounds. It was only later, after de-gowning and washing up, that she allowed herself to be comforted by Théo.

As they left their operating room together, he drew her into a deserted storage room and closed the door, dragging her into a tight embrace. 'Are you okay? None of us was expecting that.'

Connie nodded, her throat tight but her eyes dry as Théo's reassuring heartbeat pulsed under her cheek. 'Yes. Like you, I kept thinking about her husband, their anniversary, how they depended on each other and what would become of him if we lost her.'

And she couldn't help but compare herself to

Marjorie Pascal, who'd spent at least fifty years with the love of her life.

'I know,' he said, stroking her back, his lips pressed to her forehead. 'I know.'

Connie buried her face against his neck for a few more indulgent seconds, willing herself to step away because she was scared to rely on him so deeply.

'I'll be okay,' she said finally, looking up at his worried frown. 'There's never a good time to lose a patient, but it seems even more unfair at Christmas.'

Théo nodded, his hands sliding from her shoulders, down her arms until he wrapped his fingers around hers. 'Well, she's on her way to Cardiac Intensive Care now. Let's hope she recovers in time to be discharged so she can spend Christmas with her family where she belongs.'

He pressed his lips to hers in a restrained kiss, but let them sit there for a few seconds as if he needed the comfort of her touch just as much. But all Connie could think about was where she belonged. Since discovering the baby was Théo's, she would no longer be parenting alone. But would she only be included in Théo's family plans until the baby become old enough to be separated from Connie? Would she then be once more cast aside the way she'd been with her ex? Would Théo eventually move on and meet someone he wanted to invite into his life?

'Can I see you tonight?' he asked in a low voice when he pulled back.

With panic making her heart race, Connie stared into his troubled eyes, wondering if, like her, he felt they were playing fast and loose with fire. Or maybe, for Théo, everything was working out perfectly. He would have the family he'd always craved without the risk of a relationship, keeping his feelings secure. Whereas Connie... Sometimes she felt completely composed of feelings and she was terrified to examine them too closely.

'Maybe we should have a night to ourselves,' she said, suggesting the opposite of what she wanted just to prove she could go without him, that like him she too could still create some emotional distance. 'I've been a bit more tired this week.'

Only momentarily disappointed, he smiled and nodded. 'Okay. Another time, then. You sure you're okay?'

'Just shaken up,' she said, telling a partial truth as she swallowed down the lump in her throat. 'But I'll be fine.'

'I'm going to get some lunch before our next surgery,' he said, reaching for the door handle. 'Want to join me?'

Again Connie shook her head. 'I'm not really hungry. Think I might have a bit of morning sickness. And I need to speak to Jules about an admission. You go grab some lunch and I'll see you later.'

Hesitating for a second, he pulled open the door so they could once more step out of their bubble of comfort and intimacy and back into the real world.

But as she watched him walk away, her stomach twisted with fear. Bubbles were a fleeting illusion, there one minute, gone the next. Maybe Connie's feelings were out of sync with Théo's and couldn't be trusted in case they once more let her down.

The day after Marjorie Pascal's cardiac arrest, Connie was on call at the hospital. Théo knew from speaking to her that morning that she'd admitted a young man with spinal trauma following a fall and had spent half the night in Theatre performing an emergency decompression and stabilisation surgery.

Missing her and concerned that the pregnancy was beginning to take its toll on her energy levels, Théo had texted ahead then called at her apartment, his arms full of groceries.

Connie opened the door and smiled tiredly. 'Hi. Come in.'

'Let me make you dinner,' he said, placing the bags on the kitchen counter and handing her the flowers he'd also grabbed on a whim.

'Thank you,' she said, taking them in one hand

and wrapping her other arm around his neck so she could kiss him. 'I was just about to take a soak in the bath. Want to join me?'

Théo smiled, his arms tightening around her waist. 'I'd love to.' He brushed his lips over hers for an indulgent second before he reined in his ever-present desire for her. 'But I'm here to take care of you, not seduce you. Let me run you a bath.'

Connie sighed and stepped back. 'Shame,' she said, her voice playful. 'I'll just put these in water.'

In the bathroom, Théo turned on the bath taps and poured some scented oil into the water. Then, spying a box of matches on the shelf, he lit the candles in the corner of the bath and turned out the lights.

'Oh, I could get used to this,' Connie said moments later. She untied her robe and stepped into the bath, her gorgeous naked body sliding under the water.

'How's the morning sickness?' he asked to take his mind off how badly he wanted her and how his doubts seemed to be growing with each passing day.

'I think it's more fatigue than anything else at the moment.' She swirled her hands through the water, drawing his attention to her breasts, not that he needed any encouragement to stare.

'I checked on Elodie Verdier before I left the hospital,' he said. 'She's being discharged tomorrow.'

'And Marjorie Pascal is off the coronary care ward. Good news all round.' Her relieved smile made his heart beat harder. She was such an amazing woman. Caring and fiercely loyal.

'I'll just put dinner in the oven to warm,' he said, turning to leave the room before he forgot why he'd come over.

As he passed her, Connie reached for his hand. 'Come back and talk to me while I wallow.'

In the kitchen, Théo mastered his desires. Slicing a pomegranate in half to remove the seeds, he made a virgin punch and carried a tall glass back to Connie.

'So, tell me about your friends,' she said, taking a sip and moaning. 'The ones coming to the Christmas *réveillon*.'

Théo perched on the side of the bath and reached for a bar of handmade soap to wash her back, encouraging her to lean forward. 'Two are friends from university and their wives,' he said, sliding the bar over her skin, wishing it were his lips. 'Victor's sister and her husband—you met them at the wedding. And some couple friends of Tristan's that I've only met a few times but they're good company.' He set the soap aside and used his hand to scoop water over her shoulders and back, rinsing away the suds. 'I've ordered way too much food, but it wouldn't be Christmas otherwise, would it?'

She smiled and leaned back in the bath. 'So everyone else but us will be in a couple?' she asked, her voice seeming relaxed. But she kept her eyes downcast as if fascinated by her toes peeking from the water.

'Yes,' he croaked. 'Is that…okay?'

'Of course.' She reached for his hand. 'Don't worry. I'm used to flying solo. Hopefully your and Tris's friends will be a little more tactful than my family, who always grill me about my love life or lack of one over dinner. When I split from my ex,' she said, smiling, her tone light but something vulnerable in her stare, 'I'm not sure who was more disappointed that there wouldn't be a wedding: me or my mother.'

She smiled wider but Théo's responding gesture felt half-hearted as his unease grew. He'd always assumed that Connie was still happy to be alone. But it couldn't be easy attending family gatherings solo when everyone else was married with kids and also knew her history.

'Are you…nervous to meet my friends?' he asked cautiously. 'I promise they're all lovely.'

'No,' she said, seeming more relaxed. 'I'll be fine. Do…any of them know about the baby?'

Théo slid his fingers between hers, his gaze on their hands. 'Only Tris and Victor.'

She nodded. 'Perhaps we don't tell anyone else

until after the scan. I don't want to spend Christmas Eve answering awkward questions about the unusual conception and the status of our...relationship.'

'Of course,' he said, pricks of apprehension climbing his spine. 'I want you to be comfortable, Connie. I want you to have fun.' But it hadn't for one second occurred to him that others might ask his intentions towards Connie and wasn't sure how he would respond beyond *it's complicated*.

'I will. I'm looking forward to it,' she said. 'And I can't wait to see this *château* I've heard so much about.' She leaned forward, seeking a kiss. He obliged, bending down to press his mouth to hers, careful to keep it restrained.

'I'll go check on dinner,' he said, reluctantly rising to his feet. Part of him wished he'd climbed into the bath with her, but he could tell she was tired.

Later, after Connie invited him to stay the night, he lay awake long after she'd fallen asleep in his arms, his wants at war with his doubts. Could he and Connie have more than just sex? Could he take that risk and would she be ready for more? One thing was certain—he wasn't ready for this to be over yet. In fact every time he pictured the future, pictured himself and Connie nothing more than friends and parents, the crushing sense of panic he was trying to keep contained only flared anew.

CHAPTER FIFTEEN

One week to Christmas

THÉO SPENT THE week leading up to Christmas in a frenzy of last-minute activity. At work, he, Connie and the rest of the spinal surgery team tried to get through as many surgeries as possible before Christmas. He and Connie spent nearly every evening together, eating out or attending movies or classical music concerts, before stumbling back to either his or her apartment for sex that felt both increasingly vital and terrifyingly desperate, as if they knew this honeymoon period couldn't last.

Secretly, that was how Théo wanted to spend that night too. But instead, he'd arranged to meet Tris after work.

'How was Geneva?' he asked, embracing his brother then setting off for the *Métro* station near the hospital.

'Perfect,' Tris said, smiling happily. 'You must visit some time. So what's up?' Tris asked, flicking Théo an inquisitive look. Since Victor had come into Tris's life, they spent less time together, not that Théo minded in the slightest.

'I need your advice,' Théo said, still debating his plan. 'I…want to get a Christmas gift for Connie.'

Tris paused, surprised, then continued walking. 'So it's getting serious, then, is it?' he asked cautiously, his loyalties clearly torn.

Théo winced. He'd been worried about his gesture arousing Tris's suspicion. But if anyone knew what Connie might appreciate as a gift, it was his brother. And he was happy for Connie that she had such a devoted and loyal friend.

'Um… I wouldn't say serious,' he replied cagily, stepping into the nearest train carriage with Tris at his side. The doors closed and the train set off.

'But you're still seeing her?' Tris asked, wearing a small frown of concern as he clung to a vertical rail. 'Outside work?'

'Yes.' He wanted his brother's help. It seemed answering his questions was the price Théo had to pay. 'But it's fine. We've talked a lot. I'm not going to hurt her. You know me.' He glanced down at his feet. 'I don't want to repeat the mistakes of the past and, despite being married to Anaïs, there's more at stake this time with Connie.'

Tris's silence was ominous. 'And how does Connie feel? I mean, she's working with you, sleeping with you, having your baby. Are you sure you have this under control?'

'Why?' Théo asked, his paranoia finding an outlet because he wished he had it fully under control. 'Has she…said anything to you?' If Connie had reservations, she would confide in Tris.

With every passing day, Théo felt more unstable, reliving and analysing every conversation they had, uncertain of how Connie felt, despite what she said.

'No,' Tris confirmed, looking uncomfortable. 'I haven't seen her since I got back from Geneva.'

'Sorry.' Théo sighed. 'That was unfair of me to ask. Look, she's told me she isn't ready to risk her heart for another relationship right now. But, believe me, I want her to be happy as much as you do.'

Tris's frown deepened. 'But you're not looking for a relationship either, are you?'

Théo shook his head, a part of him wishing it were that simple. Given the intensity of his and Connie's relationship, he was starting to wonder if he might be ready to take things to the next level. He just needed to be careful he didn't rush too far ahead and freak her out. But then, on the other hand, he couldn't seem to get enough of her.

'We've been honest with each other from the start,' he said, hoping to appease Tris's concerns. 'If you're that worried that I'm leading her on, then speak to her yourself. I'm not buying her a ring or anything…extravagant. It's just a Christmas gift. A gesture.' Although he had considered buying her a necklace but only if Tris thought it was appropriate. 'I want to give her something on Christmas Eve. So will you help me, or not?'

'Of course I'll help you,' Tris said after a beat, still looking worried, but this time Théo suspected it was for him and not Connie.

And when it came to his own feelings, and his fear of doing or saying the wrong thing and putting the wonderful gift he'd been given under threat, Théo could offer neither his brother nor himself any such reassurance.

Christmas Eve

The weekend of the Christmas Eve party arrived in all its wintry glory. After a three-hour train journey to Marseilles followed by a short drive into the forest and vineyard-clad hills, they arrived at Château Bijou. Located outside the medieval village of Chauvel, the modest *château* nestled at the bottom of a gravel driveway and guarded by tall wrought-iron gates was a charming terracotta-roofed, ivy-draped country house made from Provence's iconic white limestone.

'Oh, Théo, it's stunning,' Connie said, admiring the green shutters framing the windows and imposing front door complete with brass knocker.

She wanted to say more, but the minute she'd

met Théo at Paris's Gare du Nord to board the Marseilles-bound train, a sense of foreboding had washed over her. Dressed casually and carrying a stylish leather weekend bag, his dark eyes bright with excitement, he'd pulled her close for a kiss that had left her breathless. She'd been quiet on the journey, terrified to blurt out the questions filling her head in case she didn't like the answers. And more than that, she was scared to examine her own feelings in case, as she feared, they were at complete odds with Théo's.

Théo collected their bags from the boot of the taxi and as they approached the front door, Tris flung it open to welcome them with outstretched arms.

'Perfect timing,' he said, pressing kisses to their cheeks. 'We've just finished putting up the decorations.'

Inside, the elegant old *château* was a little more ramshackle. The floors were uneven, the boards under the carpets creaking with age. The ceiling beams were weathered and the ancient glass in the windows was warped in places. But the furnishings and decor were warm and cosy, there was a roaring fire in the grate of the salon and Tris and Victor had done themselves proud with the decorations. Both the hall and salon boasted stunning Christmas trees and every horizontal surface a pine garland and clusters of fat, flickering pillar candles so it even smelled like Christmas.

'I've made tea,' Tris said, taking Connie's coat and scarf before ushering her to sit before the fire.

'I'll take your bag upstairs,' Théo said, hesitating in the doorway. 'I've put you in the green room, which has its own en suite and the best view.'

'Thank you,' she said, smiling but for some unknown reason feeling unsure of him all of a sudden.

'Victor has gone to change,' Tris said. 'But he'll be down soon. Then, after tea, we can all go the children's grotto if you like.'

'Sounds lovely.' Connie laughed, caught up in the excitement.

As soon as Théo departed, Tris poured the tea. 'Is everything okay?' he asked, handing Connie a cup. 'You seem…subdued.'

Connie swallowed, her carefree smile wobbling. She was torn between needing her friend's counsel and not wanting to put him in the middle because Théo was his brother.

'I'm just a little tired,' she said eventually, evading the truth. 'I don't know about you renal physicians, but for us surgeons it's been a crazy week. Everyone wants their operation before Christmas so they can recuperate with their family.'

Unconvinced, Tris eyed her suspiciously as he reached for her hand. 'I know we haven't talked much recently, what with the wedding and honeymoon and Christmas plans, but I'm still here for you, Con. You know that, right? I love my brother, but I love you too.'

Connie nodded, trying desperately not to cry. She wanted to talk about her relationship with Théo, of course she did. But she couldn't do that to Tris. It wasn't fair.

'It's a bit awkward, isn't it?' she said, trying to make light of things. 'Normally we'd gossip about our conquests, but this time is different. Besides, you're happily married now. I'll have to tell my single friends about my relationship dramas from here on.' She smiled, hoping to reassure him, hoping he'd change the subject, especially as Théo was upstairs.

'You've got feelings for him, haven't you?' Tris whispered instead, glancing at the stairs as if watching for Théo's return.

'Of course, I have.' Connie kept her voice light and breezy and her smile in place. 'We're going to be raising a child together. I care about him. We care about each other.' But she couldn't admit that sometimes, like when she fell asleep in his arms, a part of her wondered if that longing in her chest meant more than contentment.

'Okay…' Tris said, still frowning suspiciously.

'Look. You don't have to worry, okay.' She squeezed his hand. 'We're not a couple. I'm just here this weekend as a friend.'

Of course, it was way more complex than that, and Connie wasn't sure she could ever be Théo's friend. But she could keep her fears and feelings inside for a couple of days and pretend. 'Let's just have a lovely Christmas *réveillon* together.'

Just then, they were joined by Victor, who kissed Connie hello and sat on the floor beside Tris, lovingly plucking an unnoticed pine needle from his sweater.

Connie glanced away from their happiness, part of her desperate to have what her friend had found, to be part of a couple with a person who just understood her. Who was crazy about her and loved her. But she'd been there before and didn't want to be hurt again, especially now that she was having a baby. And Théo… He might understand her, he might want her physically. But beyond that, he wasn't that man.

CHAPTER SIXTEEN

LATER THAT EVENING, when Connie came down the stairs wearing a sparkly little black dress that shimmered in the twinkling lights Tris and Victor had strung in every room, Théo's mouth turned dry with lust, longing and the rumbling dread that the more he tried to hold on, the more he feared he might be losing her. He couldn't put his finger on what was different about Connie, but ever since they'd almost lost Marjorie Pascal, he'd sensed her growing distance.

She smiled and he held out his hand for hers, praying that he was wrong, that he could keep a firm hold of what they'd found.

'You look beautiful,' he said, drawing her close to brush his lips over her smiling mouth, then resting his forehead against hers and breathing in the scent of her perfume and the sheer decadence that she was there, in his home for Christmas, about to meet the friends he cared about most.

Her lovely smile widened. 'Thank you. I like

this colour on you.' She brushed her palm over his chest, admiring his favourite cashmere sweater.

Théo took her hand and led her into the salon, where a roaring fire crackled in the hearth, the scent of pine permeated the air and candles flickered around the room.

'An aperitif before the others arrive,' he said, pouring chilled non-alcoholic champagne into two flutes and handing her one. *'Santé!'* He touched his glass to hers, then, when they'd each sipped, swooped in and tasted her lips once more, lingering over the kiss as if it might be their last, but that was simply nerves.

Today, as he'd watched Connie's delight as they'd looked at the grotto, he'd come to a pretty momentous decision.

'I have something for you,' he said, leading Connie to the sofa, where he took a seat at her side.

'I thought we were doing gifts after dinner,' she said, her wary dark eyes reflecting the room's many flickering lights. 'I left yours upstairs.'

'We are,' he said, raising her hand to his lips because he was fully addicted to touching her. 'This is just a teaser. I wanted you to have it before we get carried away with good food, good company and lively conversation. Tris is threatening after-dinner games and has even created a playlist for anyone who wants to dance.'

Théo sat beside her on the sofa, his excitement

building in spite of his reservations that Connie seemed distant. He reached for the small wrapped box he'd left on the side table. Connie took it hesitantly, a small frown pinching her eyebrows together. She squeezed the edges of the cylindrical box together and it popped open. She tipped the contents into her palm, her eyes widening in surprise. 'A key...'

'Yes.' He'd put the key on a wooden keyring in the shape of a mistletoe sprig that he'd bought earlier from one of the stalls at the children's Christmas grotto.

'It's to my apartment.' Théo brushed a lock of hair back from her cheek, eager to see her reaction. 'I know it's sudden, but I want you to move in with me, Connie.' His heart pounded with anticipation and fear. But every time he thought about the future, this move was the only thing that made any sense.

She blinked down at the key on her palm, her frown deepening. 'Théo... I...'

Théo clasped her hand and she looked up. 'Hear me out, okay. I've thought it all through and it makes so much sense. We've proved that we get along, at work and in our personal lives, that we can compromise and respect each other. If we live together, we can actually raise our baby together, without always shipping it back and forth.'

Connie swallowed, something evasive shifting over her expression. 'Yes, but—'

'Look,' he interrupted, 'I don't know about you, but I hate the idea of missing out on any of the baby's milestones. First smile, first steps, first birthday. And if we keep two separate homes, one of us will always end up missing out. I don't want a broken family for us or for our little one.' He didn't want to be an absent father. And, self-ishly, he wanted Connie too, even though he might never be able to offer her everything she deserved. But then after what she'd been through, she perhaps didn't want the promise of love and marriage.

'So we'll be roommates?' she asked, once more staring at the key with uncertainty.

'No…' Théo winced. He was messing this up. 'That's not what I mean.' He hadn't imag-ined she'd want to label them and hadn't actually thought that far ahead. 'I just… I figured that as we're both in the same place when it comes to relationships but want to raise the baby together, this makes the most sense. I want to be there for you and the baby. And I can't come up with a single reason as to why this couldn't work and be the best thing for us all.'

'So would we be a couple?' she pushed, her expression guarded so he had no idea how she felt either way. 'Would we still sleep together, for example?'

Théo shrugged, his gut twisting with doubt that she wasn't as excited about this as him. 'I mean, we can be whatever you want. Friends, lovers, all of the above. We're definitely going to be parents. And given that we made our baby in an unconventional way, we can raise it that way too. We can make our own family unit, just like you said. We could at least give it a try.'

Connie swallowed, gave a small nod and glanced down.

Desperate, Théo cupped her face, bringing her eyes back to his. 'You don't have to answer now. Just think about it.' He curled her fingers around the key. 'If you decide you want to keep your own place, then that's fine. You can keep the key anyway. If we're going to be family, I want you to come and go as you please. My homes are yours and the baby's.'

Connie nodded thoughtfully. 'Okay, I'll think about it.'

Théo smiled and pressed his lips to hers. Short of her instant, delighted yes, this was the next best thing.

Just then, Tris bounded down the stairs excitedly. 'They're here,' he called, flinging open the front door to greet the first carload of guests.

Théo pulled Connie to her feet and brushed her lips with his. 'Let's enjoy *le réveillon de Noël*. I want to introduce you to my friends.'

Connie nodded and followed him into the hall. But as the festivities began, the drinks began to flow and laughter and conversation filled the *châ-*

teau, Théo couldn't help but feel there was something a little forced about Connie's smile.

In the typical way of a traditional French Christmas Eve celebration, dinner went on for hours. One course of delicious delicacies followed another and then another, until the dining table groaned under the weight of so much sumptuous food, local wine and the elbows of Tris and Théo's friends, who were locked in various animated conversations.

Connie, her stomach hollow with heartache and doubt, had barely eaten a thing. Oh, she'd smiled and chatted and pretended her heart wasn't slowly withering, but inside she grew more and more desolate.

Théo's gift, the key to his Paris apartment, felt like a poisoned chalice. On the surface, moving in together was a logical next step. She could understand why he'd asked. He was desperate for a family of his own and didn't want to miss out on time with the baby. But here, surrounded by couples in love, Connie couldn't muster one single scrap of excitement for the idea.

How could she work with him, live with him and raise a child with him while still protecting her heart? Because she'd known, the minute that piece of cool metal and warm wood had slipped onto her palm earlier, that somewhere along the line she'd fallen desperately in love with Théo Augustin.

Not that she knew what to do about it. She certainly couldn't tell him her feelings this weekend. What if he was horrified and she ruined Christmas? But staying silent also carried a price to pay. She kept going around in sickening circles.

'Bring out the *bûche de Noël*,' Tris, who was a little tipsy, called suddenly to a round of applause, dragging Connie from her depressing thoughts.

While Victor stood to fetch the traditional yule-log dessert, at her side, Théo dipped his head, his warm breath sliding down her neck.

'Come with me,' he whispered, reaching for her hand under the table.

People had been leaving the dining room all evening—to dance, to admire the trees, or fetch more wine from the cellar—so no one paid them any attention as they stood. Connie clutched his hand and followed him down a hallway to a room he'd decorated as a library and home office, one wall lined with oak bookshelves complete with a rolling library ladder.

'What is it?' he asked, gently closing the door as if Connie were made of glass and one violent disruption of the air currents might cause her to shatter. 'Do you feel unwell?'

He slid his hands up her bare arms to rest on her shoulders, his expression concerned.

Connie shook her head, terrified to tell him

the truth, but knowing she could never live with him the way he'd proposed—a clinical practical solution to ensure neither of them missed out on parenting their child. It would destroy her.

'We should go back,' Connie pleaded, taking the coward's way out. 'You're the host.'

'Connie,' he said, his frown deepening. 'Talk to me. Please. Don't...shut me out.'

Because she couldn't trust herself to be honest while also craving his touch, she turned away. 'I'm fine, Théo. I just...'

'It's the key, isn't it?' he said, his voice flat. 'I've freaked you out. I'm sorry. You don't have to accept it.'

Connie shook her head. 'It's not the key.'

Whether she accepted the key or not was irrelevant. That his only concern was that he might have moved too fast only added to her certainty that when it came to feelings, she and Théo weren't even close to being on the same page. But his gift had made her realise how badly she wanted him, wanted a proper, committed relationship. She was ready to trust him with her heart, to put everything on the line and aim for all she'd ever wanted: a loving relationship, the baby, a real family. As she looked at him now, seeing his confusion and hope, her throat ached with longing.

As if unable to stay away, he strode closer and pulled her into his arms. 'I'm sorry. My timing was off. I just... I want you, Connie. I want us to build our little family of three together. I want to take care of you and laugh with you and share all those beautiful moments in our future with you and our baby.'

Connie nodded, her eyes stinging because his words had sounded like a declaration so close to her heart's desire she almost buckled and acquiesced. 'I want that too.'

'Connie,' he said, reaching for her, pressing a desperate kiss to her lips, wrapping her in his strong arms as if he could simply hold on tight and never let her go.

Connie kissed him back, awash with all the feelings she'd been denying for days. She loved him. Was utterly head over heels. She wanted everything he wanted and more. But now wasn't the time to tell him how she truly felt. She needed to pretend for a while longer, until they were alone.

'Théo,' she whispered as his lips slid down her neck and his hand caressed her breast through her dress, 'I'm scared.' She gave him half the story.

'Me too,' he said, pressing frantic kisses over her face, tangling his fingers in her hair, sliding his mouth over hers to swallow her moans as his hands roamed her body and set her alight. 'We can be scared together. It could be perfect, Connie. You, me, the baby. We can make it work.'

Losing herself in his intoxicating words and in his kiss, Connie clung to the last thread of denial and hope that maybe, just maybe, Théo was right. It could work. They had more reasons than most to make it a success. Maybe she could give moving in with him the serious consideration it deserved before she rushed into any drastic declarations or decisions. Maybe it would help her to come to terms with her feelings and judge how Théo felt in return.

Aching for him, Connie slid her hands under his sweater and caressed his smooth, warm skin. Her tongue surged against his and her desire for this man overwhelmed her. Hadn't he proved her wrong time and time again, showing her that he was different? Hadn't he shown her what was lacking from her life, what she was denying herself because of one bad experience? Maybe it was time for Connie to be brave and trust her instincts again.

'Théo,' she moaned as he rubbed his thumb over her nipple, slipping his other hand under her dress to stroke between her legs through her underwear.

'Connie, I can't get enough of you,' he said on a strangled groan as he pressed his erection into her hip. 'I'm crazy with wanting you. It never lessens. I want to sleep beside you and wake up with you every day. I want to take care of you and run you a bath and comfort you after a bad day. I want so many things it scares me too.'

He slid his hand inside her underwear and her knees almost gave out as his kisses and his touch and his words turned her on until all she cared about was him. This. Them.

'Hurry,' she said between kisses, grappling with his belt and the fly of his trousers. This had always made sense. Surely he felt the same deep connection she felt when they were together. Surely this could be trusted, could grow into more.

She shimmied out of her underwear, backed up against the edge of the desk and shoved the hem of his sweater up until he removed it and tossed it aside.

Then he was back in her arms, his warm skin burning against hers as she spread her thighs and he leaned, reaching for her lips as she pushed his trousers and boxers over his hips.

'Connie…' He groaned, bracing one hand on the desk beside her and circling her hips with the other as he kissed her deeply, over and over until she was drunk with need and unable to think straight.

Then he was pushing inside her, filling her up, making her gasp with delight as she stared into his deep brown eyes, every part of her his.

As he crushed her in his arms, Théo's heart banged against hers. She wrapped her legs around him and dropped back her head, exposing her neck to his kisses.

'Don't leave me,' he whispered into her hair as his hips bucked and he thrust into her, his fingers stroking her nipple through her dress so she lost her mind and simply clung to him for dear life.

She loved him. She could never hurt him.

'I won't,' she cried, holding him, kissing him, staring into his eyes until they were both groaning and gasping in their search for release.

But even as she lost herself to pleasure, as they came together in a crescendo of mingled cries, of crushed-together mouths and bodies moving as one, prickles of trepidation tingled down her spine.

Panting hard, his face buried against her neck, Théo held her still as if scared to move and break the spell. Still joined as they caught their breath, Connie pulled back to look into his eyes, certain she could no longer pretend.

'I love you, Théo,' she whispered, the relief of finally admitting it euphoric.

Théo froze, his heart racing underneath her palm. Connie looked away from the confusion in his stare, pushing at his chest so he slowly withdrew and released her so she could slide from the desk.

'Connie... I...' Clearly stunned, he pulled up his underwear and jeans.

'Don't,' she said, scooping up her own underwear from the floor. 'Don't say something you don't mean. Don't patronise me. You said you wouldn't make promises you couldn't keep and I can see from your face that you're horrified.'

He reached for her arm and forced her to look at him. 'I'm not horrified or patronising you. I meant every word I've ever said to you, Connie. Why do you think I gave you the key? I want us to live together. I want us to raise our baby together. And maybe…see where this could go.'

'See where it can go?' she asked, tears stinging the backs of her eyes because she loved him, was having his baby and he was still hedging his bets. 'I know exactly where it will go, Théo. I want more than a key. More than some friends-with-benefits cohabitation. I want it all. I want you.'

'You want marriage?' he said, his expression crestfallen, as if she'd asked for the moon.

'No. Yes. Maybe.' Connie swallowed hard, humiliation clogging her throat. 'I don't know.'

How could she have been so stupid? How could she have judged this so wrong? Again. Part of her had hoped he might love her back, but he didn't, and she'd ignored the warning signs.

'But I definitely want you to have feelings for me,' she said. 'And not simply because you want the baby, because you want this figment of a perfect family, whatever that is. But because you can't live without me. Can't sleep unless I'm beside you. Can't breathe unless we're together this Christmas and every one after.'

'Connie… I do have feelings for you. I care about you. I—' His face twisted in agony, his genuine regret obvious. 'But I don't know if I even want to be married again. But I don't want to hurt you. I don't want to lose you. I can't. I can't take that risk.'

'Forget marriage,' she said, certain now that he could never love her back. 'I'm talking about for ever. You and me.' Desperately in love... How could she have been so naive? How could she have ignored the warning signs? He'd made it clear his main interest was in the baby. She'd been carried away by Christmas and his stunning *château* and the time they'd spent together.

'I...' He gripped his hair and stared pleadingly. 'I'm trying my best, Connie. I'm trying to do the right thing for us all. I'm trying not to hurt you. Not to let you down and lose you, because I've been there before. I'm partly responsible for my divorce. I thought I'd found someone I could build a family with, but I failed. I tried to be a good husband but it wasn't enough.' He stepped close and gently gripped her upper arms. 'Let's just live together and see what happens.'

Connie twisted away, unable to tolerate the burn of his touch now that her dreams were crumbling. 'That's not the same,' she said flatly, sickened by how badly she'd judged his feelings. 'Don't you understand that if I move in with you all I'll feel is resentment? I'll get hurt again. I'll be destroyed, because I can see how much you have to give, if only you weren't so scared to risk it, scared of losing it all. Don't you see?' she continued, because he was staring mutely. 'A part of you is still that terrified, grieving little boy.'

'A part of me always will be that terrified little boy,' he said, his voice dead as if she'd wounded him.

'And I want all the parts of you,' she said, defeated. 'But I can't move in with you just for the baby. I can't share my entire life and my job and my whole heart with you, knowing you're stuck in the past, holding something back, just in case.' She wanted him to want her with the same desperation.

His expression hardened. 'The past can't be changed. No matter how badly we wish it could.'

'I know,' she said, crestfallen as just how at odds their feelings were was confirmed. 'But it can be acknowledged. Feelings admitted. Isn't that the first step to learning from the past so it doesn't taint our future?'

Just then, as he stared at her dumbfounded and clueless, a raucous swell of laughter reached them from the dining room followed by Tris bellowing Théo's name.

Connie dropped her hands to her sides in defeat. She was selfishly hogging him at his own party. Throwing love bombs when it was explicitly against the rules they'd vowed. Expecting him to change the habits of a lifetime for her because she'd changed and now wanted something more.

Théo gripped her elbows before she could step

back. 'I need to see what he wants. Can we talk about this later when we're alone? I've heard everything you said, and I want to make this work. I promise you.' His stare shifted frantically between her eyes and she nodded sadly.

'Of course. You're the host,' Connie said. 'It's okay.' Stooping to pick it up from the floor, she handed him his sweater. 'You go back to the others. I might just take a moment to freshen up before I rejoin you.'

Nausea swirled in her stomach, the idea of going back to the party and pretending too much to bear.

After a beat of hesitation, Théo donned the sweater, then wrapped his arms around her shoulders and fiercely kissed the top of her head. 'Connie... I'll be back soon. Just...let me find out what Tris wants.'

With her head on his chest, she nodded but winced, knowing he couldn't see. It was obvious he was lost. She'd judged it completely wrong. Her feelings were so out of line with his: he wanted to safeguard his place in their child's life and she wanted it all.

With her heart breaking, she looked up at him. 'Go. We can talk later.' Fighting tears, she watched him hesitate then leave, her heart finally free to break in two.

CHAPTER SEVENTEEN

CREEPING DOWN THE stairs minutes later clutching her overnight bag, Connie placed her gift and card for Théo on the hall table and quietly let herself out of the house. The minute she'd been alone in her room, she'd broken down. Despite what she'd promised him, she couldn't stay a minute longer in his beautiful home, not when she'd finally given him all of her heart and he was only prepared to offer her a consolation prize in return.

Sliding into the back seat of the taxi she'd called, Connie tried to compose a message to Théo. She didn't want him to worry when he discovered her gone, but nor had she been able to face him knowing that he couldn't love her back. Not now and perhaps not ever.

After much typing and deleting, she sent a brief text.

Need some space. Gone back to Paris. Let's talk after Christmas.

With the message sent, she stared out of the window at the inky blackness of the passing countryside, every mile taking her further from Théo, further from what she'd hoped might be possible, that he'd be ready to love again. Ready to love Connie. Not just the baby. But just because he wanted to play an equal role in the raising of their child wasn't reason enough for Connie to deny how she felt and pretend.

Later, as she sat on the pretty deserted train from Marseilles to Paris, her phone finally rang. Seeing it was Tris, she picked up.

'I'm sorry,' she said before he could speak. 'I should have let you know I was leaving. I just… had to get away.'

'Where are you?' he asked, his voice tight with concern. 'Come back. Whatever happened, sleep on it. Talk to Théo in the morning.'

'I can't.' She sighed tiredly. Staying at the *château* meant once more facing Théo and she no longer had the strength. 'I'm on the train. Look… I'll explain everything when I see you next.' She couldn't relive the horrible humiliation again so soon.

'Connie,' he pleaded. 'Please tell me you're okay. I'm sick with worry. I've never seen Théo so…quiet as when he saw your message. Everyone else is leaving.'

Connie blinked, her eyes dry and gritty from

crying. She wished she could reassure her dear friend. But she wasn't okay, not yet.

'I fell in love with him, Tris,' she whispered, clearing her aching throat. 'I know…so stupid. I judged it wrong again. But I just couldn't do it. I couldn't be with him, have his baby and not feel things.'

But Théo had managed to hold back. He'd kept his heart safe the way he'd always done.

'I don't understand,' Tris said in a hushed voice. 'He said he was going to ask you to move in with him.'

'He did.' Connie sighed, the key to his apartment in her bag. 'But living together isn't enough for me. I want all of him, Tris. I love him too deeply to hang around waiting for scraps. And I know him now, know his dreams and fears. Part of him is stuck in the past, still grieving in a way he couldn't as a boy. Still terrified of losing the people he loves. And while he's still holding back, he can't love anyone, including me.'

'Can you blame him for being cautious?' Tris asked quietly, his loyalties clearly torn. 'Every woman he's ever loved has left in one way or another.'

'I know,' she whispered, scrunching her eyes closed, unable to look at her reflection in the glass a moment longer as shame burned her up. She'd promised she wouldn't leave him and then she'd done exactly that. Fled in the night. On Christmas Eve.

'I'm not leaving for ever,' she croaked, the tears back. 'Just until it doesn't hurt quite so much.'

'He's devastated, Con,' Tris whispered.

Crushing pain shot through her. 'So am I,' she said, determined to shield her heart the way Théo had done. 'But he knows I'm committed to him in a way I always will be. We'll still raise the baby together. We'll always put its needs first.'

'Even at the expense of your own needs?' Tris said. 'Your own happiness?'

Connie swallowed a fresh wave of tears. 'Yes. Because that's what parents do.'

A moment's tense silence passed during which Connie sensed Tris's disappointment. She was being cowardly. But she'd been here before and this time needed to be selfish.

'Um… I have to go,' Tris suddenly said. 'I'll um…call you later.' And then he hung up.

Théo closed the front door on the last guest, his shoulders sagging in defeat. Pain seemed to seep through every part of his body. She'd left him. Gone. Fled the *château* without a word of explanation. Without giving him a chance to sift through his thoughts and untangle his feelings and process what she'd said in the library.

Oh, he'd read her message and he understood her reasons for running after he'd been blindsided by her confession that she loved him. But what he couldn't understand was why he was still standing there instead of chasing after her and begging her to give him another chance.

As he re-entered the kitchen, half dazed, Tris hung up the phone.

'Was that Connie?' Théo asked, foolish hope rendering his throat tight. 'Is she…okay?' Maybe she'd changed her mind and was on her way back to him. Maybe they could work through this and start over.

Or maybe he'd simply got what he wanted all along—his precious emotional safety. So why was the full-body agony only getting worse with every breath?

Tris nodded guiltily. 'She's on the train back to Paris.'

Théo scrubbed a hand down his face, a sense of inevitability causing him to slump despondently into a chair at the rustic farmhouse kitchen table where Tris and Victor had opened a bottle of whiskey and had obviously been nursing nightcaps.

Hadn't a part of him always known that this was how it would end? Hadn't he lived his entire adult life waiting to be rejected or abandoned? And he'd somehow doomed himself to relive history repeating itself over and over again.

'I poured you one,' Tris said, sliding him a glass.

Théo gripped it, just to give his hands something to do, but he knew he wouldn't be able to swallow a drop. And he wanted a clear head to make sense of how things had gone so badly wrong.

Perhaps sensing some serious soul-searching was about to go down Victor stood and touched Tris's shoulder. 'I think I'll grab a shower before bed,' he said, casting Tris an encouraging look before leaving the room.

'I can't believe she left,' Théo muttered to himself after another moment of tense silence, debating jumping in the car he kept at the *château* and driving all the way back to Paris.

'Can't you?' Tris challenged loyally, shooting him a dark, accusing look that then turned sympathetic. 'I told you to be careful with her.'

Théo pushed his glass away. 'I thought I was being careful. I never made her any promises beyond being there to help raise the baby.'

'Connie's the toughest woman I know,' Tris said. 'She doesn't really need your help, or your promises. But she loves you anyway. Did she tell you that?'

Théo nodded miserably, closing his eyes on a wave of nausea, picturing Connie's beautiful face as she'd bravely told him how she felt. As she'd given him all of herself, given him everything he wanted but was too scared to reach for in case it seeped through his fingers like water.

'Do you think it's true?' he asked his brother, his voice a pained croak. Could she truly love him, as messed up and emotionally cautious as he was?

Tris frowned. 'Why do you doubt it?'

Théo swallowed, his gut churning. 'Because I've been here before and it all went wrong. Because she promised she wouldn't leave me, only tonight, but she left anyway,' he snapped, frustrated with himself for allowing Connie to walk away thinking he didn't care and feeling as if he might throw up.

'Because she's scared, just like you,' Tris said, glancing worriedly at Théo. 'Scared to take a chance on love and get it wrong again. To be hurt again. For the past three years she's told herself she's safer alone.'

'I know.' Théo hung his head, his mind spinning in circles. 'And tonight, I proved her right,' he whispered, standing to pace the kitchen. There was too much energy boiling inside him to sit still. How could he have done the one thing he'd wanted to avoid: let her down and hurt her? When Connie had given him everything.

'I can't believe you let her go,' Tris said, shaking his head.

'It's…complicated,' Théo said with a wince at how pathetic that sounded. 'It's not just about us and our feelings. We have to think about the baby…'

Remembering how Connie had accused him of only caring about the baby, he groaned in frustration.

'It's always been complicated,' Tris pointed out. 'That doesn't mean you should give up.'

'We're not giving up,' Théo argued, helplessly. 'We're choosing to put the baby first.'

'You're choosing fear,' Tris said with an unsympathetic scoff. 'Both of you.'

Théo stared at Tris, his heart lurching at how lost he felt and how Tris seemed more emotionally together.

'She said you're stuck,' Tris said, his eyes wary. 'Said you didn't grieve properly when we were kids. Is that true?'

'I... Probably...' Théo swallowed, the heart he'd kept carefully protected all these years cracking open so all the fear and doubt in him spilled free.

Connie was right. Some part of him had never properly processed what he'd lost as a child. He was terrified of losing people he cared about, people he loved. That explained why he'd behaved so abominably tonight. He loved Connie, desperately, so his fear was at its pinnacle.

'Is it because of me?' Tris whispered, his thumb rubbing at a divot in the scarred tabletop. 'Because you had to take care of me because you're older?'

'No.' Théo paced back to the table and rested

his palms flat. 'It's because of me. Because Connie is right. I'm terrified to let anyone close in case they leave me. Like Maman and Mémé and Anaïs and now Connie. But it's too late,' he said, certain that alongside the fear his broken heart had exposed were other feelings. Enormous feelings he'd spent weeks denying. 'I love her too,' he finally croaked, closing his eyes against the burn in his chest. 'I have for weeks. I've just been in denial.'

'Of course you do. So tell her that,' Tris said excitedly, as if it were as simple as speaking those three little words.

'I wish I could. I wish she were here.'

After a few tense moments of silence, Tris cleared his throat and stood. 'I love you, Théo, but you know you don't need to take care of me any more. I'm an adult and I'm happy and I want the same for you. I think that's what Connie wants too.'

Théo turned wild eyes on Tris, needing his younger brother's wisdom, a part of him right back there to that scared little boy. 'But what if I tell her, if I try to grab what I want and lose it again anyway? I don't think I'll survive, Tris. Not losing Connie…'

Tris tilted his head in sympathy. 'You just have to take the risk, like the rest of us. Look around,' Tris said sadly, shrugging. 'It's Christmas Eve. A time to hold your nearest and dearest close. Connie is gone and if you don't tell her how you really feel about her, you're unlikely to get her back. What scares you more? That you try and maybe fail, or that you don't try at all and never know if you might have found the perfect love, the perfect family you've always wanted?'

Théo nodded, his lumbering, battered heart restarting as if shocked back to life. 'You're right. How did you get to be so wise?'

'I had an amazing brother and role model,' Tris said softly.

Théo swallowed, the love he'd tried to contain pouring out of him. Love for Tris and their precious little family. Love for his child, but most of all for Connie. Maybe if he caught up with her, told her how he truly felt, he could win her back, persuade her to give him another chance. Persuade her to come back home. Maybe they could work at this terrifying love thing together.

With his mind instantly clear, he marched across the kitchen. Snagging his keys from the hook by the back door, Théo briefly hugged Tris. '*Joyeux Noël.* Enjoy the *château.* The fridge is stocked, there's plenty of wood for the fire and I give you permission to raid the wine cellar.'

'Wait. What are you going to do?' Tris called as Théo flung open the back door and marched out into the freezing cold.

'I'm going to Paris. To find Connie and tell her how I feel.'

'It will take you all night to drive,' Tris called after him, but Théo was already sitting in the car and gunning the engine, which was sluggish from the sub-zero temperatures.

'I'll take the train,' he yelled, slamming the car door. Then praying for a Christmas miracle, he floored the accelerator, sped down the gravel driveway and took the road to Marseilles.

CHAPTER EIGHTEEN

CONNIE ONLY MADE it as far as Avignon on the train before she came to her senses and changed her mind. Tris was right. She'd thought she'd bravely given Théo her whole heart, but she'd still been scared, had still held a sliver back because she didn't want to be hurt all over again and run. But Théo would never deliberately hurt her, and she'd broken her promise and left him the way he almost certainly had expected her to because of his past.

Rushing to the opposite platform in the railway station, she boarded the next Marseilles-bound train. Frustration formed a tight ball in her stomach. The train just wasn't moving fast enough. She needed to go back to the *château* and be fully honest with Théo. She needed to give him the time he'd asked for and seriously think about them living together. She needed to tell him that she would always love him, even if he couldn't love her back.

In despair, she dropped her face into her hands.

Tris had been right. Théo had lost every woman he'd ever loved. And in acting out of fear, in clinging to the desire to protect that last piece of her heart, Connie too had run out on him. On Christmas Eve!

With trembling hands, she fired off a text to Théo, hoping he might still be awake even though it was after midnight and now officially Christmas Day.

Never should have left. I'm coming back. Let's talk. Please.

She'd just about given up on a reply when her phone pinged with an incoming text.

This is Tris. Théo is on his way to find you but left in a hurry without his phone. Where are you?

Connie practically howled in agony, her heart thudding painfully.

On the train to Marseilles. Should I change again and head to Paris after all?

Where was Théo headed? Surely he wouldn't drive all the way back to Paris alone?

To Connie's relief, Tris's reply came swiftly this time.

No! Get off train at Marseilles and make a wish that you intercept him there. That's where he's headed.

The thirty-minute journey back to Marseilles felt more like a thirty-hour-long haul. Plenty of time for Connie to list, alphabetise *and* re-arrange her endless regrets in descending order. How could she have behaved so stupidly, allowing her fears to stand between her and everything she wanted? How could she ever have convinced herself she could be content with so little? Faced with a kind, honourable and passionate man worthy of her love, her feelings just wouldn't stay contained. And a man like Théo was worth fighting for.

As a recording finally announced Marseilles station, Connie grabbed her bag and headed for the nearest exit. The automatic doors seemed to take a year to slowly glide open, then she was out on the platform and hurrying towards the station exit.

That was when she saw Théo, running her way, his face lighting up when he spied her. She froze, her bag sliding from her hand as he ran faster. She couldn't believe they'd found each other.

'Connie,' he said, panting hard as he gripped her shoulders. 'You came back.'

His relief was palpable. Connie nodded, everything she wanted to say to him stuck in her throat, which was clogged by her overwhelming feelings of love.

'I'm sorry,' she choked out. 'I should never have left. I know I broke my promise.'

'No, *I'm* sorry,' he cried. 'I should never have given you a reason to leave.' As if he couldn't be without her in his arms a second longer, he wrapped them around her shoulders and held her close so she felt the rapid thud of his heart against her cheek.

Connie clung to his waist and breathed him in. He smelled like burning candles and pine needles and Théo. 'I was scared,' she admitted, her joy that they were reunited, that they'd found each other, bubbling up.

'Me too,' he said, prising her far enough away so he could peer into her eyes. 'You were right about everything you said. Every word. I'm so glad you came back.'

'I only left because I couldn't face seeing you again,' Connie rushed on, trying to explain why she'd left, 'knowing that I might have judged this so badly, but—'

'No,' he said, cutting her off. 'You didn't judge it wrong. I was just too terrified to say or do the wrong thing because I didn't want to lose you. I couldn't survive losing you, Connie. Not you.'

'But that's just the thing, Théo,' she pleaded. 'I came back to tell you that it's okay. You don't have to be scared. We'll always be a family. You, me, the baby. You could never lose me. I'll never leave you again, I swear.' Even if she had to find contentment as his friend.

'Connie,' he said, swiftly kissing her lips, his stare wild with passion. 'You don't understand. I love you. I want the same things you want. I want for ever with you. I want this Christmas and all our future Christmases. I just panicked earlier because I've messed this up before and it would kill me to lose you. Not just because of the baby, but because I want to spend the rest of my life with you. You're everything I want. I've loved you for weeks, I was just in denial. I'm sorry.'

Before she could speak, he covered her mouth with his. Their lips slid together, breath mingling as they grabbed at each other in obvious mutual desperation. Connie's heart soared out of her chest and she smiled against Théo's mouth.

'You love me?' she asked when she'd pulled back, smiling for joy.

He tunnelled his fingers through her hair and cradled her face, his stare adoring. 'I love you so much I ache whenever we're apart. I watch you sleep. I fantasise about all the places I want to take you on holiday. I've bought you far too many Christmas gifts because I just couldn't help myself, and if you're going back to Paris tonight, that's where I'm headed too, because I won't be able to sleep unless it's wherever you are.'

'Théo…' Connie blinked, happy tears seeping from the corners of her eyes.

'Please forgive me,' he said, pressing his lips to her forehead. 'Please give me another chance to prove to you that I am ready to love you with every inch of my terrified heart. Please let me try to be the man you deserve, because I promise you, unreservedly, that no one will ever love you harder than me.'

'Okay,' she said, laughing through the tears that stung her eyes. 'But there's nothing to forgive.'

'Okay?' He smiled wider. 'I'll take okay,' he said, his mouth returning to hers. And for a long time, despite the cold and Théo's lack of a coat, they kissed on the platform, not needing the excuse of mistletoe, because they had their love for each other instead.

Until Théo had Connie safely back at the *château* and snuggled by the fire with a warm drink, he couldn't fully relax. He'd driven back from Marseilles station with one hand on the wheel, the other hand holding hers, a goofy smile on his face as he'd looked over at her every few seconds. But having almost lost her tonight, he wasn't taking the risk of physically letting her go again.

Now, sitting by the fire in the salon with his arms wrapped tightly around her, he drew her even closer and buried his face against her neck. 'I love you,' he whispered. *'Joyeux Noël.'*

'Joyeux Noël.' She smiled up at him and snuggled closer. 'I'm sorry if I ruined the celebrations.'

'You didn't. You being there made the celebrations everything.' He stroked his fingers through her hair, simply enjoying the beat of her heart against his. 'Everyone rushed off to catch midnight Mass in the village. Besides, *le Réveillon de Noël* is about family and you are my family, Connie.'

Connie pulled back and picked up the gift she'd carried in from the hall table. 'This is for you. I want you to open it.' She held the box out to him, her eyes bright with excitement and love that choked him.

'You first,' Théo said, handing her the gift he'd purchased with Tris.

Smiling his way, Connie untied the ribbon and prised open the box, her face lighting up as she examined the contents and gasped. 'It's beautiful, Théo,' she said, pressing her lips to his then gently fingering the delicate gold chain inside.

'Try it on,' he urged. 'I'll do it up for you.' Taking the necklace from the box as Connie swept her hair aside and turned around, he draped the delicate chain around her neck. 'Tris helped me choose it. So if it doesn't fit, we can blame him,' Théo said, fastening the tiny clasp and then pressing his lips to the back of her neck.

'It's perfect.' Connie turned and smiled. 'I love it. Thank you.'

She kissed him again. They couldn't seem to stop kissing or touching each other.

'Now open yours,' she urged excitedly, pushing the gift his way.

Théo didn't really want to let go of Connie but nor could he deny her a single thing. He opened the box to find a digital photo frame inside. The frame surround was a stylish dark wood and when Connie pressed the *on* button, the display screen came to life with a photo of the two of them together at Tris and Victor's wedding. Instead of smiling at the camera, they were smiling at each other, their expressions so obviously enamoured, Théo couldn't believe it had taken him so long to recognise his feelings for this incredible woman.

'It can hold thirty thousand images,' she said, scrolling to the next photo she'd uploaded. It was Tris and Victor on their wedding day, and then a shot of Tris and Théo as boys, their beautiful *maman* in the centre. 'So there's plenty of space for photos of the baby and any others you want to display.'

With his chest aching that she understood him so well, Théo scrolled back to the first image of him and Connie. 'This one is my favourite for now,' he said, drawing her close for another kiss. 'Thank you. It's a perfect gift. You obviously learned some skills from the gift master.'

She laughed and he swooped in for a kiss he

almost couldn't bear to end. 'I can't wait to fill it with happy memories of our family.'

'Neither can I,' she said, reaching for her bag and pulling out his apartment key. 'I want to move in with you, if the offer still stands.'

Théo cupped her face. 'Do you really need to ask? I've never wanted anything more than to wake up with you for the rest of my life.'

With her eyes shining and smiling, she held the key above their heads, the mistletoe keyring dangling above them. 'Shame to pass up on an opportunity,' she said with a seductive smile.

'I will never need an excuse to kiss you,' he said, knowing he would love her for ever. Then, because it was Christmas, and Connie was the best gift he'd ever been given, he pressed his lips to her smiling mouth.

EPILOGUE

Christmas Eve one year later

WITH BABY ELISE asleep after her feed, Connie carefully handed their precious daughter over to Théo.

'I'll just put her down,' he said, looking at their daughter with wonder then gently kissing the baby's forehead before heading for the nursery in their Paris apartment. Connie watched through the baby monitor as he lovingly laid four-month-old Elise in her crib and sighed with contentment.

Théo was the perfect father. Loving, attentive and fun. Somehow, watching him be the wonderful parent she'd instinctively known he would become, Connie fell a little deeper in love with him every day.

'She's so utterly perfect,' he said, sliding next to Connie on the sofa and, with his arm around her shoulders, drawing her close. 'Just like her *maman*.'

Connie smiled, raising her face to his for a kiss. 'And her *papa*.'

'She's so wonderful, I think we should make more babies, don't you?' Théo teased.

Connie beamed indulgently. They had of course already had this important conversation many times in the past year so he knew they each wanted another child to complete their little family.

'One more,' she said, resting her head on his chest. 'And maybe in another year.'

Théo held her close and kissed the top of her head. 'Of course, we can make the next one in the traditional way if you like.' He placed his index finger under chin and pressed his lips lazily to hers, slowly savouring their kiss, the heated look in his eyes making her shudder deliciously.

'Let me just finish my drink and then we can practise,' Connie teased and snuggled closer. 'Because practice makes perfect.'

The rumble of Théo's chuckle vibrated through his chest as Connie relaxed in his arms. The fire crackled in the grate, the warm air carrying the scent of pine. The instrumental Christmas chill music softly played in the background and as Théo's heart gently beat beneath her cheek, Connie had never felt so content.

After a moment, he shifted, producing a small box from underneath the sofa cushion. 'There's one more gift for you,' he said, handing her the velvet box, his dark eyes tender.

'Théo…' she whispered, her heart rate spiking excitedly as she sat up and stared at the box. She prised open the lid and gasped, her stare flying back to Théo's.

'It can mean whatever you want it to mean,' he said about the stunning diamond ring. 'I want to marry you if you want to be married. I want to spend the rest of my life with you and grow old by your side, married or not. I want to raise our family with you and I'll never stop loving you, Connie. Just be mine.'

Connie laughed ecstatically, although her vision swam with happy tears. 'I want all of that too,' she said, pulling the ring from its velvet cushion.

Théo took it from her fingers and slid it onto her ring finger. 'So will you marry me, Dr Dubois?'

Connie threw her arms around his neck and kissed him, her heart soaring with love for this incredible man who'd taught her that love *was* worth the risk. 'I will, Dr Augustin.'

Théo's radiant smile squeezed another drop of love from her heart. '*Joyeux Noël*, my love.'

'I love you,' Connie whispered, embracing their always simmering passion as she brushed her lips over his. 'Happy Christmas.'

* * * * *

If you enjoyed this story,
check out these other great reads
from JC Harroway

One Night to Royal Baby
One Night to Sydney Wedding
Manhattan Marriage Reunion
The Midwife's Secret Fling

All available now!

Get up to 4 Free Books!

**We'll send you 2 free books from each series you try
PLUS a free Mystery Gift.**

Both the **Harlequin Presents** and **Harlequin Medical Romance** series
feature exciting stories of passion and drama.

YES! Please send me 2 FREE novels from Harlequin Presents or Harlequin Medical Romance and my FREE gift (gift is worth about $10 retail). After receiving them, if I don't wish to receive any more books, I can return the shipping statement marked "cancel." If I don't cancel, I will receive 6 brand-new larger-print novels every month and be billed just $7.19 each in the U.S., or $7.99 each in Canada, or 4 brand-new Harlequin Medical Romance Larger-Print books every month and be billed just $7.19 each in the U.S. or $7.99 each in Canada, a savings of 20% off the cover price. It's quite a bargain! Shipping and handling is just 50¢ per book in the U.S. and $1.25 per book in Canada.* I understand that accepting the 2 free books and gift places me under no obligation to buy anything. I can always return a shipment and cancel at any time. The free books and gift are mine to keep no matter what I decide.

Choose one: ☐ **Harlequin Presents Larger-Print**
(176/376 BPA G36Y)

☐ **Harlequin Medical Romance**
(171/371 BPA G36Y)

☐ **Or Try Both!**
(176/376 & 171/371 BPA G36Z)

Name (please print)

Address   Apt. #

City   State/Province   Zip/Postal Code

Email: Please check this box ☐ if you would like to receive newsletters and promotional emails from Harlequin Enterprises ULC and its affiliates. You can unsubscribe anytime.

> **Mail to the Harlequin Reader Service:**
> **IN U.S.A.:** P.O. Box 1341, Buffalo, NY 14240-8531
> **IN CANADA:** P.O. Box 603, Fort Erie, Ontario L2A 5X3

Want to explore our other series or interested in ebooks? Visit www.ReaderService.com or call 1-800-873-8635.

---

*Terms and prices subject to change without notice. Prices do not include sales taxes, which will be charged (if applicable) based on your state or country of residence. Canadian residents will be charged applicable taxes. Offer not valid in Quebec. This offer is limited to one order per household. Books received may not be as shown. Not valid for current subscribers to the Harlequin Presents or Harlequin Medical Romance series. All orders subject to approval. Credit or debit balances in a customer's account(s) may be offset by any other outstanding balance owed by or to the customer. Please allow 4 to 6 weeks for delivery. Offer available while quantities last.

Your Privacy—Your information is being collected by Harlequin Enterprises ULC, operating as Harlequin Reader Service. For a complete summary of the information we collect, how we use this information and to whom it is disclosed, please visit our privacy notice located at https://corporate.harlequin.com/privacy-notice. Notice to California Residents – Under California law, you have specific rights to control and access your data. For more information on these rights and how to exercise them, visit https://corporate.harlequin.com/california-privacy. For additional information for residents of other U.S. states that provide their residents with certain rights with respect to personal data, visit https://corporate.harlequin.com/other-state-residents-privacy-rights/.

HPHM25